THE GREY HARE

A ROMANCE OF THE DANISH FIELDS

THE GREY HARE

A ROMANCE OF THE DANISH FIELDS

by

SVEND FLEURON

FARRAR & RINEHART, INC.
NEW YORK   TORONTO

CONTENTS

THE GREY HARE

A ROMANCE OF THE DANISH FIELDS

"The old mother hare bravely held her own"

THE GREY HARE

CHAPTER I

THE FAMILY

AT the end of March a mild wind blew for a few days from the southwest; then it veered round to the east and grew sharp. The weather was hard and wintry and the mornings both gloomy and cloudy.

Snow fell.

But the hare's form, in its heap of clay, was tolerably comfortable.

An old mother hare had borne her leverets there. She had lain on a piece of land that had been turned over with pick and shovel and then abandoned.

The form was down at the back of the mound, over-shadowed by a fringe of thick, yellowish grass. It was hidden by a big cotoneaster bush, brown with the cold, and some tall stems of wild chervil covered with empty seed-pods.

The east wind whistled and blew the empty seed-pods about, beating the angular stems wildly against each other; there was a seething and boiling among the dry stalks; they rustled and rattled.

The tumult increased, the sky grew black, and hail pelted down. The lapwings cried over the mother hare's head, whirling round and round in mad, merry circles, then mounting on steady wings upwards to the grey dawn. Larks trilled on every side and little yellow-hammers—a knowing hen bird and a pert and lively

3

little cock in his finest plumage, that looked as if it were made of the scour-thistle's first golden petals—bustled twittering about looking at the nest through the fringe of grass.

In spite of the biting blast, in spite of the snow and the hail showers, the birds were announcing their spring nuptials. In their unimaginable ecstasy they forgot summer's toil and winter's want, and sang as if happiness beyond all understanding were awaiting them.

Muddy water washed the edge of the form where the mother hare lay with her new-born leverets; for there were winter floods in the depressions between the mounds, with regular waves rising. Each time a wave beat upon the edge of the nest a cloud of muddy spray would fly upwards.

The old mother hare was doing her best to deal quickly with the situation. Her first-born, a droll little grey-brown, downy fellow, already lay panting and making valiant efforts to get his breath.

He was not, as a little rabbit is, wrapped in warm, protecting down from his mother's breast, but, wet and unprotected, he sat under a yellow tuft of grass and let his mother lick him dry. His round head, with its still undeveloped muzzle, his lustreless eyes, looking as if they were made of tin, and the whole of his crouched, shivering body had as yet no consciousness of being in the world. The little creature had come into that world so recently that it could have gone out of it again without understanding what had happened.

Meanwhile the mother hare quickly regained her strength and settled down over her litter to feed them. At once they made great efforts to suck, and strength came rapidly in the little creatures as they nursed.

The snow shower was over. The sky had cleared a

little, but it was still rather cold. The hare remained sitting over her leverets until they had sucked their fill.

A hare is an extraordinarily good mother. For a time she cares for her new-born little ones, then springs up and goes to an exposed form in the middle of a field. She knows something of the scent which proceeds from her and which attracts the dog and the fox, and she will not expose her helpless little ones to danger. Besides, she needs rest in order to recover completely.

The sun went on its way behind the grey-black curtain of the clouds. Soon snow showers fell, covering the earth with white, but a minute later it disappeared again.

The new-born leverets were unharmed by the weather. They were cold and they shivered; but they were cold without realizing it, and their shivering kept up the natural heat of their bodies. It also excited their nervous systems and called their senses to life, so that they began to see, hear and feel. There was a murmuring and a whistling above them. The piercing wind nipped their extremities. Boisterously it roared out their christening psalm and blew strength into their nostrils. They took in the air with deeper and deeper breaths. From being heavy, moist masses they became light, elastic balls. They could jump and stretch and move about. They knew that they were alive! Grass moved, tree-like, before them; they perceived its still stems and long, pendant blades. Their little yellow home was separated in their minds from the grey sky. A mole that, with amazing speed, built up its hill in front of them was the first phenomenon that they observed. Slowly they emerged from the drowsiness of their new-born state, until the time came when they sank back into strengthening sleep.

The sun went on its way behind the grey-black cloud

curtain. Morning was followed by noon, afternoon and evening.

The old mother hare remained awake in her furrow. She felt light and active. It seemed that for a while she had forgotten her leverets. Her thoughts were fixed on a mangel-wurzel that had fallen from a cart. She wanted to gnaw it, but she forgot it when a longing for her little ones suddenly came over her. She sought them out and settled down over them. They drank until they were satisfied and, animal-wise, she felt a momentary tenderness for them. Then she sprang away and resumed her accustomed night life, guarding herself from the sneaking marten and the cunning weasel. Again she forgot her young—until, with dawn the mother-instinct reawakened in her.

The second day passed.

The changeable March weather was over. Everything was quiet and the air was clear and cool.

Sheltering under a clump of grass on which the rime lay, the little leverets crouched together for warmth. They had begun to make rapid progress. They were swift of foot. They knew that they had mouths, and how to wash those mouths with their forepaws. They were also fully conscious that they had stomachs hanging beneath them, and when those stomachs were empty their mouths wanted to suck and their tongues to lick.

In the late evening, as they lay on a bed of grass, cozy and warm, something soft and warm settled down over them. They nuzzled their little noses into their mother's coat and drank.

On the third morning the air was full of promise. On the far horizon swam a bluish veil of mist. A snail, awakened by the spring, was wandering through the grass, showing that a swift change in the weather was soon coming.

The leverets sat dead still, pressed against the earth, their little ears along their backs. With wondering eyes they gazed at the big cotoneaster bush and the wandering snail, which were just within their range of vision.

They heard the cry of the lapwings and the trilling of the larks. The lowing of cattle and the squealing of pigs came to them from the village of Bjaerg, and the rumbling of carts and the trotting of horses was audible from the neighbouring road. A dog began to bark violently, and the echo of five of the smith's mightiest hammer blows sent a series of sonorous notes drumming through the air. The leverets heard them, they heard all the sounds together as a distant and continuous murmur, but no individual sound made any particular impression on them. They didn't know what they were, and couldn't distinguish one from the other.

The whispering of the wind in the coarse meadow grass over their heads, and the sudden rustling among its dry blades when the old hare brought them warmth and milk, was all they noticed and understood of the world.

There was much for them to learn if they were to get to know their way about. The most important thing they had to realize was that they would not be provided for much longer. Would they grow up into hares, or would they only be grain for the great mill of life and quickly go to feed the crows and foxes?

When they were four or five days old, it came suddenly into the head of one of them to look at his paws. It was the first-born leveret. He was a queer, fluffy little fellow. The paws had hitherto only wanted to rub his muzzle, but now all of a sudden they wanted to move along.

He had happily come to know his clump of grass, and he wanted, very naturally, to have a little change. With the innocent confidence of the novice he set forth slowly and cautiously. Soon he came upon a little patch of tightly curled moss. The delicate colour of the moss, and of all the green things about him, kindled a spark of the joy of life in his eye. Out of the patch of moss grew a stem of the wild chervil. He rubbed his chin and neck against it and peeped at a little sprouting leaf near its root. He sat down and contemplated the curly leaf, which seemed to beckon to him . . . .

The colour of the little leaf was a lighter green than the moss. He didn't know the reason of this, but the longer he gazed at the curly leaf the more hungry and thirsty he became. He had to go up to it and sniff it and taste it. It smelt pleasant and tasted good—and so all of a sudden the curly leaf was gone.

After this he became bolder. He seldom stayed still, but more and more frequently made adventurous excursions from his clump. He did not know much yet about hopping; he was not very careful; he just followed his nose along the ground, making his way by means of his disproportionately long back legs. He had to get used to this means of locomotion and to slipping lithely in and out among the long blades of tough grass on the mounds. For him the grass was a thick wood, and for a time an impenetrable one, which often barred the way to a hare of his undeveloped powers. But at length he made his way through and reached the top of the mound, whence he saw a little open space spreading out before him.

From his point of vantage he saw, in the middle of the open space, an enticing tuft of green, which gave out a delicious smell. His front teeth suddenly ached to gnaw that tuft. Suddenly a little field-mouse bustled out of its hole and with quivering nose began to sniff at the curly sprout. The leveret felt he must go and gnaw too. Both he and the mouse began by nibbling a little, and immediately agreed that the tuft tasted good.

Thus little Josse made his first acquaintance with a carrot top.

He passed the whole evening nosing about in the neighbourhood of the carrot tops, and when dawn came the next day he returned to them, bringing his sister Hopsy with him.

Once more the sun of a day travelled across the sky. The red light of the sunrise coloured the clouds and filled the sky with long violet streaks. Clouds floated over the field where the carrots grew. The withered grass on the mound blushed to a warm purplish-yellow hue.

But day was the sleeping time of the little long-eared leverets.

When twilight drew near Josse woke up and grew lively again. All at once he became aware that he could see a long way. There was a new, much larger field of tufts a few hops to the side of the old one. He must go and taste what was there. But the smell that blew across from these tufts was not pleasing to his nose, and when he sniffed at the plants his mouth didn't water a bit. He hastily let go of the first thistle that lifted its head from the low carpet of grass, for he was already dainty —so dainty! He was on his way home when he met his little table companion of the day before. They sniffed at each other with delight, then went off and ate young carrot tops again.

When the sun went down, Josse was filled with an ecstasy of joy. After sitting for a while rejoicing, he suddenly made his first real leap. The mouse was so frightened that it ran back into its hole. But Josse stayed where he was and made leap after leap, quicker and quicker. At last he became so skilful that he even leaped over a bush!

After this feat he felt himself possessed by an incomprehensible self-confidence. He sat down on his hindquarters and, lifting his forepaws from the earth, gazed slowly right up into the sky. When he felt his balance was secure he shot up again into the air as high as the stiffness of his unaccustomed muscles would allow—and he noticed with pride that he had very nearly leaped above the top of the grass.

He was already a regular young hare and could use his legs. It was strange that when evening came they always wanted to go out and hop and jump. It made him glad—but the only thing he couldn't understand was why Hopsy didn't always want to come with him. When he began to run she, as a rule, held shyly and cautiously back.

The open space which he knew soon became too small for Josse. He wanted to see the world.

Along by the far side of the field, where the fine, tender green tops of the carrots were soon gnawed off, the grass grew thickly. He ventured into it. Here he noticed a grey-brown lump that stood so firmly in its place that even the strongest blast could not stir it. Tests with his teeth and nose gave him no information about the lump, but it made a great impression on his nose and teeth! The big, hard stone awakened his inborn curiosity.

In the evening he had to go to it and satisfy his curiosity. He rubbed his little muzzle against it and it seemed that a cold breath came out from it. He kissed it with his little moist, quivering snout and it scratched him hard. Not even with his sharp little chisel-like teeth could he make any impression whatever on it. So he let his paws try what they could do with it. At once the stone and his paws seemed delighted to discover that they could rub tenderly and fervently against each other; he danced on the flat top of the big stone, and when he was tired he sat down and looked for the first time out over the wide world—over the tops of the mounds that rose up round about him like huge brown clumps of grass.

The week passed quickly.

Under the warm, golden starlight the sides of the mound gleamed dark and moist. Moisture lay on the blades of grass and from the stems of the wild chervil heavy, gleaming drops fell. It was real growing weather. Mild and spring-like blew the southwest wind straight into the little leverets' faces.

Their mother had just been with them and they were filled with well-being. She had been noticeably damp, almost wet, for she had come to them, as she went from them, through flooded fields in order that her scent might not be followed.

Josse had not allowed himself to be deceived by the dampness and at evening he did not feel inclined to dance on the stone; a lucky thing for him and for his more careful sister!

The lapwings were about in the darkness. One cried "Pee-wit" and another fluttered down the wind. The night was alive with the sportive, playful birds.

All at once their merry cry changed; it became plaintive and mournful, and there was a note of foreboding in it.

The lapwings' lament floated far and wide over the fields. The cause of the flock's uneasiness was a lean old vixen that, without the least idea that she was the subject of observation, was slinking along a field path. The vixen had whelped a day or two before and wanted to find something to eat which would put strength into her. A nest full of lapwings' eggs had but whetted her appetite. Now she wanted to come upon something alive.

She made her way down to the ditches and smelt about among the mounds. She came quite near, passing close by the clump where the leverets crouched. Each time she came near them they noticed her strong, indescribable smell. She stood still and turned round and round sniffing about among the grass. Eventually the fox slunk away again into the darkness.

At last it was dawn. As the day advanced the southwest wind grew stronger, spreading the mists of night over the day. It blew strongly over the open fields. It came to the grass on the edges of the mound and laid it flat, so that it stood out like the flying mane from a horse's neck. It paused for a moment in its wild career, sank down into the valleys with a sigh and a moan, and then, whistling and roaring, swept upwards to the hills. It whispered among the clumps of grass and murmured with a thousand tongues amid the dry blades.

A big, feathery-legged hawk was floating over the mound. Its great wings went up and down in long, even strokes; in their full swing they almost came together beneath its breast, pressing the air powerfully backwards under its belly and tail. This movement suddenly ceased and it remained for a moment on steady outspread wings. A white-spotted male bird came up and stopped by the side of its brown mate. But they did not remain long together in this dignified flight, for with wide, sweeping strokes of his wings the husband flew away over the fields towards the forests of Sweden.

At the same moment a flock of crows swung soundlessly out of the grey twilight. They came from the opposite direction; the brisk breeze of dawn bore them along towards the light. They were out early looking for their breakfast and hoped to find a good, warm meal ready for them! With their heavy crops they swung forward clumsily through the air. Their heads, black-capped, were continually in motion, as if to give their round, sharp-sighted eyes a chance as they sent a scouting glance downwards. Now and then there came a harsh, startling cry, a solitary salute to the morning. Whenever there was the likelihood of anything to eat near at hand, they began to quarrel at once.

They were big, grey-breasted crows, with wings like shovels and stiff, pitch-black tails that projected out behind them like long sticks.

Josse's little table companion, the mouse, was down from the top of the mound like a shot and disappeared into his hole. Josse himself had a feeling that made his paws very quiet. They were of one mind with his back and perfectly still. Hopsy had separated her ears and had let them droop down at the sides of her head. She was the one who thought the least and fared the best. Brother Lab, the third and last-born leveret, who up to the present had never been outside his clump of grass, hadn't the least idea of what was going on.

The crows hastened on their way until they caught sight of the white-spotted hawk. At once they made a circle in the air round him and with hoarse, angry cries drove their rival away.

Meanwhile the brown hen hawk had ceased her musing. On outstretched pinions and flight-feathers that looked like separate fingers, she hovered over one particular spot. For a moment she was poised there quivering, with down-bent head, then she swooped down over one of the hillocks and circled vigilantly round and round in search of the day's food.

The crows were gone and the leverets picked their way back to their native clump. Josse's little paws at once began to think of the dancing-stone.

It was just the time when the old mother hare was ready to feed her leverets and she felt full of tenderness for her young. She was already on her way in from the fields, without a suspicion of what was awaiting her.

The big bird of prey, fluttering from hillock to hillock, caught a glimpse of something hairy moving among the yellow tufts of grass. Maybe it was nothing but an illusion, but it *might* be a hare's ear—and, like the experienced hunter she was, she would go over and take a good look.

But the old veteran had come just at the right moment! With the hair on her back bristling, she made herself look very fierce as she ran round and round the big hawk, pretending that she would rush in on it from behind. She leapt over the bird, scratching it with her forepaws, giving the impression that a hare was furnished with claws and a beak.

So the old mother hare bravely held her own, until at last the feather-legged one had to take to its wings and soar up into the air once more.

The old mother hare stayed with her leverets and gave them a meal. Then she made haste to get away before the sun rose. She sought the form she had scraped out for herself in the fields, where she knew she could lie in peace. She fell asleep as soon as she reached it and enjoyed her day's rest with an easy conscience.

It was a windy but sunny day, full of sprouting, swelling force.

The earth had begun to smell extraordinarily fresh and pleasant. Josse noticed that the greensward was warm and that the air about him was balmy and full of light. This acted on him as it did on his mother: he dozed and slept.

A high, crystal-clear stream of sound kept on continuously over his head. For a long time he paid no attention to it, but at last he heard it, looked this way and that, and peeped with one eye in the direction from which the sounds came. Thus for the first time he looked at the sky. It was blue, with bright, white spring clouds, and he mistook the lark's singing for the voice of the sky.

The bird dropped down to its tuft of grass. It came down silently. When it soared again and its song sounded and trilled over him again, he, Hopsy and the already sleepy Lab had each gained a little new experience.

The lark was an old, worldly-wise cock bird, familiar with the earth and its inhabitants. It knew every possible kind of knoll and tuft in the fields; it knew from dearly bought experience when it was safe to come down and what changes in conditions took place with each change of the moon. It had learned all that, just as the little long-eared ones were learning it now in the spring. A lot of helpless little leverets that skulked on the earth in a clump of grass did not interest the lark at all—but Hopsy trembled when the bird made its sudden descent, and her eyes grew twice as big as they were before.

When Josse next woke he took note of a new creature which with glistening plumage flew along by the edge of the flooded fields. It was obviously different from the lark; but like the lark it could both walk on the earth and fly in the air. All at once it became quite big. It extended its skin and ran and leapt and hopped in the wind. Josse saw it time after time and soon became familiar with its dive in the air over his head: he learned enough of its language to understand that it called itself "Pee-wit."

He was never tired of looking at it.

Three or four skips. Then a halt, neck outstretched, looking about. Isn't that a worm? Yes, it is. Pounce! Again a skipping run. A start, and the head held a little on one side. Isn't there a spider under that leaf? There is! Now then, quick! A peck, and it's gone! Between the catches a continual looking up and spying. . . . An upward dash and a couple of circles in the air and a shrill cry that all the world may hear!

In the evening, just before sunset, Josse saw the lapwings again, quite close at hand. The blue of the sky gleamed on their shoulders, and the bright green of the grass shone on their wings. The sides of their faces were as white as his mother's belly and they had long, projecting tufts on their heads.

They were never quiet; they cleaned and pecked at themselves. They pecked round about them when they were on the ground. They shrieked and turned somersaults and played foolish pranks when they were in the air. You couldn't mistake the creatures once you had seen them.

But the day did not come to an end before Josse discovered that there were many other living creatures besides him and his brother and sister. He suddenly heard a new voice just above his head. "Tee-ee! Tee-ee!" it said.

This voice, which was strong and haughty, was not

continuous like the lark's warbling, nor did it spurt forth, fountain-wise, like that of the bustling lapwings. There was something more precise and, as it were, commanding in its tone.

Josse couldn't see what kind of a creature the voice came from.

It had been an eventful day.

Was it that the day had been so full of incident—or was it that he had grown and could now see better with his eyes and hear better with his ears?

Twilight was already falling. Evening had come again.

It was a spring evening and the air was fresh and clear. There were no clouds, but the sky was bright with the many colours of sunset. High up it was blue. Then came light greenish clouds, between the blue and the violet. Lower down was the area of the sun, that went from pale to deep gold and then to fiery red—and in the distance, clear and distinct against the pale, gleaming horizon, was a big forest.

The black earth was still blacker in the sunset light—and where trees that stood crowning a slope were outlined with all their fine maze of branches against the sky, the first stars twinkled pale and timid. After a good day's work the southwest wind had gone to sleep.

Josse was aware of the witchery of the twilight hour. His teeth wanted something juicy to gnaw and his eyes could now see far-off things distinctly. The blinding light of day no longer made the distant clumps of grass on the other mounds indistinct.

When the sun sank and the earth drew its garments of darkness closer and closer about it, the young hares became more and more lively and confident. They crept out from their clump of grass and each took its own way amid the uneven tufts, diving through the big ones and jumping over the little ones. They raced in a series of gay, careless hops across the open spaces where the thistles and carrot tops grew. Then they came to the long grass, a thicket of stems that often barred their way and dropped cold drips of dew on to their noses. In the evening they all went up on to the flat stone to dance and enjoy the view over the lime pits. It seemed to them that they had grown so extraordinarily tall that they could spy out the whole neighbourhood. Josse, who was the boldest of them all, peeped at the big windmill which, in solitary majesty, stood at the lower end of the lime pits. Its great staring eye made him quite giddy. He had never seen so tall a *bush!*

A little to the other side of the dancing-stone a narrow path wound through the grass. Feet found this path almost as quickly as eyes. The path was level for hopping and easy to move along—so said all four soft little pads. It led along the edge of the lime pits and soon widened into a field path, along which the loose-jointed little legs could gallop still faster than before.

Lab, struck by his brother's example, seemed to be quite animated in the evening, dizzy with all the new things he was doing and seeing. He followed close in Josse's steps. But Hopsy was left behind. She stared cautiously through the grass by the dancing-stone.

The field path shone bright, glittering with billions of frost particles. But that made no difference, when one felt so full of strength!

It went on in a zigzag, with sudden turns and twists. Soon the brothers came to a standstill and sat down with heaving flanks and saw a strange moon rise from their grass clump in the distance. They were soon rested. They washed their faces like cats and carefully brushed their whiskers.

Josse, the downy one with the dancer's legs, was the wilder of the two. Besides his love of jumping he was endowed with an extraordinary curiosity. If there was anything near his nose he absolutely had to sniff at it and find out what it was. He had already found out that such investigations were sometimes well worthwhile.

Now he spied a long, deep ditch in the ground. The urge for discovery possessed him, and with little, cautious hops he slipped down towards it, without knowing what he wanted there. His eyes said: "We can scarcely see!" But his paws would go forward. They were quite unruly. The joy and strength of the winter-bound earth crept up through them.

Lab only followed him for two or three hops. Then he thought better of it and turned hastily home along the field path. But Josse ventured further and further across the field, and the rime of night and the mist of evening lay damp on his coat. It was so pleasantly soft to walk on there in the ditch; the loose earth moved and gave as he went; it yielded, scattered and was soft under his pads . . . it was something completely and altogether different from the dancing-stone! The earth smelt fresh; it had the smell of the wild chervil's sprout and the haylike scent of the dry grass—blended with an aromatic tang.

Closely and intimately the ditch shut him in. His back, that had never before gotten so much pleasure at being outside the protecting clump, felt an extraordinary sense of safety at the bottom of the ditch. Loose stones gleamed before him and white roots, turned up by the plough, stuck out from the sides in many places. There were many projections and lumps of earth that got in his way, of which his sensitive whiskers warned him, so that he avoided them, climbing up and making his way past them.

Once, when he was climbing over a huge obstacle, a wide prospect opened up before him, and his ardent desire for movement surrendered unconditionally to the impression it made on him. He *had* to sit still and meditate when he looked out over the ploughed field. The ploughed land was like an immense expanse of hares' backs that gleamed in the light mist of the spring night, as though it were greasy!

He left that field behind him and came into another deeper ditch, with gleaming water at the bottom. When he had thoroughly investigated and carefully tried the depth of the water, which he found to be disagreeably cold and wet, he went back and explored his first ditch exhaustively.

It ran across a field, and he followed it a long way. His back had become a bit uneasy. This was travelling in earnest. Suddenly a thick pole seemed to rise up out of the earth and walk stiffly and solemnly to meet him. He threw himself, in fear and abasement, flat on the ground and remained lying there for a long time; but the pole never moved at all, nor did it show hostility in any other way, so at last he regained his confidence and went towards it. He thought it must be a bit of strangely thick darkness until he had hopped round it several times and sniffed at it—then he had *discovered* it.

In a similar manner he discovered a dike which crossed the ditch. He followed it and came to some clover, and he did his duty by its many young sprouts. He had now nearly been along three sides of a square, and was by no means clear that he hadn't lost his way, but the clover had been sown by a machine and fortunately for him the rows led along parallel to the fourth side. Instinctively his feet followed one of the rows, and so he came happily to the field path again, at the far end of which Hopsy and Lab greeted him as if he had been a new Columbus.

He had had enough for one evening. The moon was high in the sky, and it was strangely clear and silent round about in the fields. It was obviously best to go to bed—so they all three together crept under a little willow tree and found it a new and snugger lair.

They passed a good night. It would be a long time before the vixen came to this corner. She found so much prey in other places, and had recently been fortunate enough to catch a big, white-spotted hawk, which had been sitting quite tired out behind a hedge with two dead crows in its claws. The fox was not accustomed to luxury, so that coup had given her enough for the time being. The little leverets could be at peace.

The dawn was at hand.

The three little things under the willow had long noticed the coming of day. They had hopped out into a little open space, where each of them was feeding among the newly grown scour-thistles and the luxuriant fresh-smelling grass. Josse went in front and the others followed. They went after him without any inducement, for the warm, soft thing that, morning and evening, was accustomed to sit over them and feed them had not turned up the whole day and night, so that they were both hungry and thirsty. While they were enjoying the sunrise, a black shadow suddenly hid the sun from them. They were startled by a shrill caw. Hopsy, who had raised her ears, and who was sitting cleaning the wet dew from her whiskers, first noticed the danger. Her forefeet were on the ground in a moment, and her erect ears fell and lay along her back. She turned over with her legs in the air, and instead of being a living leveret became a little dead lump of earth. Josse did the same. Lab followed suit.

The eager caw came again. The leverets knew from its tone that they were threatened. They felt it more than any other sound they had ever heard and were filled with terror and anguish. Their pulses hammered; their little sides heaved; even their sensitive ear-lobes quivered.

The red light of sunrise now shone in all its brilliance over their heads, and made their eyes glitter like quartz in a rock—until the shadow again flew up and glided between them and the sun.

"Caw, caw," came the sound. It was not quite so savage as before, its tone was softer, expressing joyous surprise, but the leverets distinctly felt a waft as of night's cold breath. They crouched close against the earth, making themselves so small that they looked not like clods of earth, but like tiny, insignificant lumps in the ground.

For a moment the shadow left the air.

When that happened a little life came back into the leverets' bodies. Their legs twitched impatiently. Suddenly the legs resumed their duty and, in a twinkling, took the little animals into the shelter of the willow. But they had scarcely arrived under cover when the air was filled with the roar of the storm. They heard a great tumult of flapping wings and saw one shadow after another glide over them. "Caw, caw-aw," came loudly above them, and one caw sounded even more savage than the others. The air was filled with the sound of cawing.

Sunrise had given place to golden sunlight, and on

every side day was increasing. It peeped in curiously through every tiny aperture in their green hut of leaves.

What was taking place at that moment outside, none of them could see. They just lay still and listened. Suddenly they heard the patter of a hare's pads, striking the earth hard. Quickly the legs galloped away, quickly they returned flying, leaping, with the cawing hard after them. Now they were nearly at the leverets' shelter, and the leverets heard the sound of puffing and blowing which they recognized.

The old mother hare, who had forsaken her young for so long, had at last felt moved to return to them. She had heard the crows' battle-cry and had now appeared to protect the leverets. The crows had come at an inopportune moment for themselves. Had they come the day before, or in the evening, she would have been quite oblivious that she had a little Josse, a little Hopsy, and Lab. She had been running about then, thinking of other things. But now—now her motherhood flamed up, wild and self-sacrificing; and instead of a mere hare such as the crows understood, they found a small tiger that thought nothing of springing at them.

But the winged robbers were endowed with a devilish cunning. They knew how to work together, and by so doing, how to secure a larger prey. They were accustomed to doing that with owls, and even with the big, feather-legged hawk. They would conquer the mother hare now they knew where the leverets were. They would use their usual tactics, trying to draw her away and keep her away while the others, remaining behind, would break in and secure the booty. But she was far too old and clever to let herself be fooled like that.

What cawing and raging went on outside!

There were crows in the air and crows on the ground.

They surrounded the hares in their leafy shelter. On the threshold the fearless old mother stood erect with open mouth and paws in fighting attitude ready to do battle for her young.

Josse didn't know how it happened, but the nearer the tumult came, the louder shouted his paws that he was mad to remain sitting here, that he should trust himself to them and they would take him to a more peaceful place, where he could take his day's rest and chew the cud in peace. His little brain had a hard fight with his fleet paws, but all at once, when his mother, retreating before the black and grey marauders, trod on him with her big hind legs as he lay there, he let his paws have their way and took to flight.

His example was infectious. The leverets scattered in every direction and scampered over the open space into the grass and clover, while wild caws sounded behind them. But so suddenly and with such whirlwind speed was the sally made that the enraged robbers were quite taken by surprise. They were too long in starting the pursuit, too long in swooping downwards, and they could not unite quickly enough round one of the leverets. The leverets sprang forward and were away before them into the green rye and young clover and into the wide lime pits with their thick, dry grass.

So the crows flew back to the old mother hare, in the belief that there were more leverets in the shelter. But she had the courage of a lion, had the old one! She danced a wild war-dance with them, in the course of which there was snorting and cawing, tearing with fore-paws and the menacing nearness of wing and beak. Each time a crow alighted she was on it like a cat, so that it had to hurry back into the air. Then suddenly she made

a sally which drew the crows right away from the
willow tree.

The more experienced of the birds, seeing that the
game was lost, resumed their interrupted morning excursion in silence and indifference. The younger and more
excitable ones, however, took a longer time to calm
down, but as they resumed the attack, the flock thinned,
and when the last one suddenly perceived that he was
quite alone, and was calling "To the attack! To the
attack!" before an old, wild-looking she-hare, he was so
taken aback that his voice stammered and died away in
a throaty "Caw-aw-aw."

The leverets went on their way. They twisted and
turned, slipping along through grass and ditch, clump
and tuft. Hopsy was the best traveller—that is, she was
the most sure of what she had to do and in what direction she had to run. With her ears laid along her back
and crouched low, she spied out her way like a mouse,
choosing her path through the grass where the stems
were highest and thickest. Lab, who in the heat of the
fight had received a scratch from a crow's claw right
across his forehead, had become so lively and alert that
he had no further doubts as to the use that he ought to
make of eyes, ears, nose and limbs. He scampered from
refuge to refuge like a grasshopper, just as if he were an
old hand and had already done a world tour through the
grass.

But it was Josse who ran the hardest and strongest.
He went on and on, letting his active feet find the way,
and followed it. And the feet followed an immemorial
law of nature inherent in them, a law that was mysteri-
ously inherent too in all Josse's little body. They ran
round in a circle! This very fact was Josse's salvation,
his good fortune; so wisely had Nature ordained it that,

just because of that law, he came at last, without knowing it, to the one place in the world which he knew
better than any other—to his home!

The battle was over by this time. The crows had led
his mother cunningly away with them.

He knew the place again: the low-lying fields, the
broad field path, the clover growing in rows—the dancing-stone! There was the open space with the gnawed-
off carrot tops, there lay the mound in the shelter of
which he had been born and there the willow stood and
swayed in the wind. He greeted it with joy. All the
other grass and straw he had been through had been to
him like drops in a sea, he had only noticed them as a
close, protecting *something;* but not one flower, not one
bit of earth had meant anything to him. Now at last he
was home—and he dived into the dry grass and sat down
confidently to wait.

And as Josse went, so went Hopsy and little Lab.
They all ran round in a circle and, coming from every
direction, ended up in their home form without knowing
how it had happened. Soon the old mother hare was on
her way to them. They heard her signal—a peculiar,
loud, rattling sound which she made with her long ears
—and they nestled up against her and relieved her anxiety for them as they fed.

Now they knew the crows' caw as before they had
come to know storm and snow and the evil odour of
the fox.

Hopsy had also made the discovery that paws are
good and can be very useful. She needed that experience. It wasn't enough for her just to keep cover and be
cautious in her excursions. In spite of all that one may
meet with an accident.

Josse learned from the attack of the crows that the

world wasn't just a young carrot. He must be careful where he jumped to; he had enemies who were waiting to hurt him—and his back had certainly been right when it had so often felt itself neglected in favour of his dancing paws. Rather dejectedly he decided henceforward not to break new ground before he had meditated and thoroughly thought things over. He came quickly to the conclusion that his paws had proved themselves real heroes!

As for Lab, he was so confused that he didn't know what to make of it all; yet he was the one who should have had the most fruitful experience, for he had been under fire! The hurt on his forehead should have knocked into his brain the realization that the cawing of crows was not only connected with fear and noise, but also with beaks and claws.

It wasn't so easy to make Lab wiser.

The days became lighter and the nights milder. The wind had grown gentle and warm. The mound was covered with tender bright-green grass. The grey pools had become blue, and the funny little toads on the mound began to send forth their high clear trilling. In nearly every pool there was a little "triller," floating with all its four legs extended. They were there while the day was warm and mild, but suddenly disappeared when the sun set. A high blue sky alternated with a heavy rain.

Josse and his brother and sister no longer sat together, but apart, each in his own green clump. There was something among them that stirred them up and kept them awake. One morning Josse saw that in the place where he had been lying during the night, and which had proved very uncomfortable, a big, strong dandelion had grown up. It had been the stalk of this which had been irritating him the whole night! Now its pale green leaves stood up and sent out a sweet, herbal, spicy smell.

The smell of the plant pleased Josse. His teeth ached to bite it—once more the earth had been kind to him and had given him a new source of food and drink.

By the evening everything round Josse's bed was green with these plants.

The leverets saw their mother less and less. It seemed that her affection for them had ended in the fight with the crows. Now that they could eat by themselves and suck the sap from plants, let them try to be independent! As she ceased feeding them, she seemed to become more forgetful, volatile and light-minded, till suddenly she realized that she hadn't time to devote her accustomed period to her leverets. She lost interest in them.

One day, when the earth was aglow with sun and alive with the growth of spring, the leverets were surprised to hear a rustling among the chervil stems. The scent made them aware of their mother's presence, and Josse and his brother and sister emerged, each from his tuft. Lately they had drunk nothing but plant milk; they scarcely remembered their mother. They had met her indeed, but noticed that another hare followed her, which, as soon as it perceived them, laid its ears back and struck out fiercely with its back paws.

This was Lepidus, their father, a wicked, crafty old buck hare! He had a big head with great staring eyes and a disproportionately large back and hind quarters.

Ever since the leverets had come into the world, he had passed night after night running about with his long legs in the wet grass; he was seeking his own children in order to kill them, so mad was he with jealousy.

Now at last the little things were before him. They came boldly up to him. Simple little Lab at once began to use the "finger language" of the ears. Lepidus rushed in among them, scratched them with his forefeet, so that the fur flew from their heads, and snorted wildly and noisily with his big, quivering nostrils, frightening them terribly. His fury knew no bounds; his jealousy increased. The leverets felt as they had felt on the morning when the crows attacked them.

They turned and ran headlong, and he after them! They dived into grass and ditches and lurked in cover among thorns and stones. Far from their native place and from the lime pits he hunted them. He gave them a lesson as to how to start in life: duck your head, take cover, never show yourself in the daylight, avoid all things that move on the earth and in the air. Everything is against you, nothing is for you—even your own father is your enemy!

Josse ran and Hopsy ran and Lab followed after as well as he could. It was a Day of Judgment!

Josse came to a stop in a field where the earth had been broken up and lay in clods. He crouched down between two clods which were close together.

A big, stern man was walking about the field, plough-ing it with a team of great, powerful horses. Other ploughs followed, drawn by horses which were nearly as big and just as strong.

The man was Farmer Jens Tyrbag, out doing his spring ploughing with his sons.

Josse was too preoccupied to observe anything, other-wise he would perhaps have recognized in old Jens Tyr-bag's furrowed, dirty face certain traits which might have reminded him of his own wicked father. As it was, he merely hastened to make himself insignificant. He put his grey back under the shelter of the clods and only when it was well concealed did he begin to think. Shelter gave him safety and restored the use of his senses. There he sat and looked. He observed the horses and the furrows made by the ploughshares and listened to man's speech.

A big thoroughbred St. Bernard dog lay over in a kennel by the fence. It was as big as a three-months-old calf and had a mouth like a lion. It was guarding the nosebags and its master's well-worn, shiny, greenish coat: treasures the value of which it well understood. Hour after hour it kept watch with half-closed eyes and with its big head resting on its forepaws. When one lapwing and then another gambolled too near its nose it slowly raised one red-rimmed eyelid and showed a dreamy eye.

By nature Kora was aggressive and had, in her time, been inclined to go up to people and show them her teeth and let them feel the weight of her body, but under Farmer Tyrbag's strict and vigorous training she had become as gentle as a lamb.

The ploughing went duly on, the work progressed uninterruptedly and steadily. There was no unnecessary word spoken and no pause in the ploughing—only a "whoa" and a "gee-up" to the horses.

Kora arose and, lazily stretching her sun-warmed limbs, lumbered off for a little turn round the field. She took long, sober strides, with a powerful swing of her heavy flanks, accompanied by a sweep of her tail from side to side. She went slowly and indolently forward, interesting herself chiefly in sprouting plants and heaps of manure.

Josse scented the animal coming from the windward side, and he had the same sensation in his back as on the night when he had scented the fox. "Quiet now!" whispered his back.

Kora went on, sniffing as she went. Soon she was down in the ditch, and then she entered the field. She approached Josse's clod and scented him. Suddenly it became pitch dark in Josse's earthen cell and a moist, cold nose came down on top of him.

That gave him a start; but the heavy clods round about him gave him back his confidence. Now was the time either to use his paws (but they were too tired), or else to adopt Father Lepidus's course of action, of which he had so recent a recollection. Instead of taking to his heels he began to make short, sudden jumps up at the dog's nose. He snorted and spluttered like a kitten and, flapping his ears noisily, he scratched with the sharp nails of his pointed forepaws.

Josse bluffed and got the better of his enemy for the first time in his life. He experienced the greatest satisfaction when after his fierce defiance Kora's great jaws loosened and she trotted off.

Kora was very good-natured where small creatures were concerned, and she never touched a hair on the back of a mouse or a rat. Her aggressive nature only took note of what was bigger and stronger than herself.

It helped Josse, too, when Kora's severe master, who always preferred to see things in their places, shouted "Hi, there, dog!" and bade Kora hurry up and lie down.

She started off at a trot back to her nosebags, running with bent legs and dribbling mouth, and setting her heels deep into the earth. She carried her bushy tail like a hook standing out behind her.

The rest of the day Josse spent in peace between his clods. The evening came and the sunset's clean, pure colours appeared over the fields that awaited the coming of spring. Breezes blew gently through green rye and grass and whistled among the hawthorn bushes in the dikes and in the willows. Larks sank down and disappeared into their night quarters in the young clover, and from the mysterious depths of its mass of stems heavy, black beetles appeared one by one and, buzzing, took to flight. The yellow coltsfoot shut its flowers.

Jens Tyrbag and his sons unharnessed their horses and rode home. Deep stillness fell over the fields. . . .

From that day forth the leverets saw their mother no more.

CHAPTER II

JOSSE'S SCHOOLING

JOSSE had the appearance of a timid, startled creature. When one or another inhabitant of tuft or field
looked at him he behaved as though he were extremely surprised and confused. This was only one of
the many tricks inborn in him.

He had a good share of natural shrewdness, also speed
and never-failing vigilance. Hopsy had shyness, caution
and cunning, while robust Lab had been born with a
convenient little mixture of everything. But to all of
them nature had given splendid gifts: cheerfulness, live-
liness, and a matchless appetite.

They were just a month old and looked rather like
little clods of earth. One saw nothing of their heads but
the eyes, which were set like smoke-coloured pebbles,
one at each side of their clod-like bodies. The long,
characteristic hare-face, with the deep furrow on the

33

nose, was quite absent as yet. They might easily have been mistaken for little round bull-dog puppies.

But every day they grew: whiskers, body, ears, short forelegs, long back legs, and their little hare faces too.

Their surroundings grew still more quickly. They couldn't keep up with them. Fields, meadows and ditches, seeds and plants were all about them. The rye already hid the lapwings. The wind sent waves through it, so heavy and dark was it. The spring-sown grain showed its light, pure, early green on the soil of the smooth fields. When the sun shone the fields gleamed a golden green. Lapwings hatched securely around. Moles built their soft little hills, and Josse, who was very fond of the sun, often scratched out a day-form for himself in the middle of one of them.

Along the hedges and by the fences lingered a remnant of drifted snow, left over from the winter's storms. Its stiff crust showed on projecting mounds of earth. Last year's grass and the brown earth were still visible, but day by day the new green things grew thicker and stronger. Besides the wild chervil and dandelions came burdock, even sorrel and speedwell. All wild-growing things sprouted again either from new seeds or from their last year's roots. On the mound, where strange plants grew, there sprang up a big St. Anne's wort, with thick, stiff leaves, growing as it were out of a stone.

Formerly Josse had been able to hop all over these plants, but now he had to go under or through them. He couldn't go round everywhere he liked, but had often to move patiently forward in short hops, like Hopsy. This cost trouble and effort and he came to value paths and boundaries.

But the earth became dearer and dearer to him as the spring advanced. The days were a dream, the nights a delicious adventure. It was a joy to be alive, to feel oneself a ruler over all things that were rooted in the ground and bound to one place. The many delicious plants he met with on his way—did they not stand there in their delightful daintiness and offer themselves to him? Did they not stand there, so temptingly decked in all the colours of the rainbow that his long gnawing teeth watered? Pilewort, groundsel, and oh! the dandelion. Red clover, medick and wild pea, yolk-yellow, apple-red and grape-blue, alluring colours that were like fruits to him.

And as one happiness after another leaped towards him he became more and more enchanted with life. Life's joy spiced every plant he ate and his paws tingled. He often got so excited that he had to jump.

He and his brother and sister still kept to the neighbourhood of the old lime pit which lay unused with its many mounds and hollows like a stormy sea that had been suddenly solidified into land. In the depressions between the mounds, from which all the winter floodwater had now disappeared, grew the harebell, shrinking under the sun's blaze. Only the thistle and the coltsfoot and the spicy potentil could send down their roots there. But on the top of the mounds, where the rich dug-up earth had been spread, all the weeds banished from the fields flourished luxuriantly. Here grew the charlock, the giant silicule; bindweed like woodbine, mugwort like poplars, and the docks, with their seed-hung, brick-red tops, soared like little village church-steeples to the clouds.

From the lime pits the leverets ventured further and further out into the landscape. On along by ditch and broad hedge they went. They looked out across the adjacent fields and meadows, then turned back, so frequently had they met with serious trouble in their voyages of discovery. They sat and let their many small experiences mature, learning through their long sensitive ears a little hare's most important art, namely, always to be in close contact with the surrounding world.

Sitting there, they arrived at the certainty that there were many other creatures besides themselves that made their way through the fields, and that far away upon the hill, where the big white stone cone towered, dwelt a colony of strongly smelling, erect creatures. All kinds of trouble and noise came from there. It was beyond Josse's and even more beyond Hopsy's understanding how those creatures up there could endure one another. Even one of them was enough to make young hares take to their heels in the utmost terror.

In the late evening, when they ventured near to the big hill, they heard angry "bow-wows" and plaintive lowing and bleating. Then suddenly this storm abated and became a mere breeze that little by little died away on the night.

They were seldom together now, these little, long-eared folk. By nature they were solitary, and by day always sat alone and quite often far away from each other. Only from time to time, generally late in the evening or in the early grey of the morning, it happened that they met. Josse came upon Lab or Hopsy now and then, or sometimes both. Then Lab and he played, while the more staid Hopsy looked on.

When the desire to gambol had gone out of their little legs they all three sat together in an intimate cluster and talked to each other in their sign-speech, with tails and ears.

Josse's tail was like a crayfish's, that could smack up and down. It was white on one side and black on the other . . . short, flat, and plump. Lab's and Hopsy's tails were much the same.

When they were filled with delight or quivered with eagerness or wrath, their tails kept up the conversation. If, on the other hand, a mood of a more complex nature was to be expressed, the ears took up the tale.

One ear in front and the other behind meant: "I'm all right and enjoying my food." One ear erect and the other inclined meant: "I'm in doubt and don't rightly know what to take." Both ears up, but sloped a little backwards, expressed the most complete indifference. Close together, but held a little forward, they gave the idea of surprise or said something like "You idiot!" Finally, both ears raised straight up in a combative horn betokened: "There is danger all round. Be careful! Look out!"

Josse was the one who best knew the sign language of his race, and he could vary it much more than the other leverets. But then he was always on the move and rampaging about for nights on end, so he saw and heard a great many things and therefore always had a great deal to talk about.

Hopsy found a place in the grass and kept to it, only coming out to feed. Lab had to have a companion if his paws were to get going. He very seldom made an excursion by himself. But Josse had to leap and rush about. Like a Jack-in-the-box, he was always ready to be up and away if anybody meddled with his lid.

There were many such meddlers in the fields. He would have several adventures in one week.

The heat of the sun poured down from a cloudy sky through the misty air. Cows in the cowsheds mooed, for they could smell the grass. After April's rough, cold spring weather, May and June cast the mantle of summer over the land. Clover grew high, the grass was bright green, chestnuts, birches and beeches put out their leaves, and the bees, that had long been hungry and frozen, hummed a summery song of content. The little birds, which since their coming had had to hide themselves in hedge and thicket, now sped about all over the place. Daisies opened their white flowers and dandelions their yellow ones. The birds of summer hatched out, flowers unfolded and beetles came forth by thousands every minute. The prudent starling, who had alone foreseen the time for egg-laying, was seeing to its business in the trees and on the scrap heaps. A pair of lapwings out in the spring corn had had their first nest destroyed by the spring ploughing; magpies had stolen their second clutch of eggs from them, and now they had a violent and irresistible urge once more to trust a further brood to the unreliable earth.

Innocent little Josse, too, felt his own peculiar pleasure in midsummer. Though he had experience enough to know that he shouldn't venture forth in the day, he did what pleased him most. In his simple, grey garb he even sported in the green fields. So greatly did he come to love the sun that without the least regard for safety he lay at full length on one side. His white breast and tummy had to enjoy the sunrays too! There he lay, showing white in the young clover.

As he was at the height of bliss, a sound came to his ears that seemed hostile to him. His feet made short work of bringing his brown-grey back to a place of refuge, and just as they did so two long-tailed birds alighted just where he had lain. Their heads and necks gleamed like a pitch-black sod of peat from a bog, but on their wings and along their see-sawing tails shone the windy blue of the pond. Each had a dazzlingly white jacket on its body and over its shoulders, and the black, white and blue were sharply and clearly divided from one another.

Josse knew the magpies well from his earliest days. They had built their domed nest of sticks high up at the top of a poplar on the nearest farm. For a week before Josse's birth the cock magpie had acted both as burden-bearer and carpenter. Later on he had had to be labourer and mason, and had plastered the bottom of the nest with clay. This was why the pair had once come to the pool before Josse's mound, where they found suitable material, but then he hadn't had a chance to observe them.

After his adventure with the crows Josse had never felt at ease when magpies were near. Something in their nature always reminded him of those grey robbers.

The magpies had finished building long ago. The pair was about to hatch eggs, and early and late they were collecting the necessaries for this proceeding. The ingenious birds investigated everything, stuck their beaks down into mouse holes, and rummaged about on mounds.

Josse sat, well protected, in his refuge. He had just satisfied his back that all was well when a pair of thick, black-scaled legs strutted into the clover tuft near him. The faint green light in his cramped refuge, which acted so soothingly on his frightened mind, suddenly changed into a glare of blinding white sunrays. Then the old dispute between paws and back broke out. The dispute was not of long duration. Both the long-tailed ones fell simultaneously upon him. They pulled his ears hard, they pecked him with their beaks, and they scratched him with their toes and claws.

Instinctively he gave his agile paws their way and flew rather than scampered out of the tuft. His paws hammered the earth beneath him. Plants and flowers fled by him. He ran as fast as he could, the magpies' hateful pursuing cry ringing in his ears. He deserved to be hunted for being fool enough to leave his lair in the daytime and showing himself openly in the light to all.

Something whizzed behind him and a pair of black, swiftly flapping wings were above him. He heard the dull sound of the wind's pressure against their taut feathers. A moment later the wings were back again, beating him at one side; he felt the slap of a stiff, snarling flight-feather against his sensitive whiskers, and a sharp whistling sound hurt the drum of one of his ears. With that he jumped to one side. The magpies rose up into the air and swooped down again suddenly past his nose, so close that he smelt the strong breath of the pied carrion birds. They were making for his eyes. Of all that was his they wanted them first. He mustn't be able to see what they did later!

There was a boundary ditch close by; he dimly glimpsed its green streak. On one side of it rose the low, erect wood of ears of spring-sown corn. On the other grew wild flowers. But right in the middle, between corn and flowers, ran an uncovered groove, a regular little track for all the creatures of the field, for beetles and ants and field-mice and little, simple, scared hares. Oh, how even and pleasant it was to hop there! He rushed onward. . . .

Wild, spicy camomile, lovely, swaying brome-grass, white-flowered wild chervil grew up to the very edge of the groove. He saw them and knew them in the midst of his wild race. A worse way little Josse couldn't have taken. He should have concealed himself in the ditch and crept into the first mouse hole he came across, but

his paws were so very weary that they couldn't make
that clear to him. He came out into a flat, level field.

The magpies followed him. With quick, whirring
strokes of their wings they sped along and kept behind
him at a fixed distance whence from time to time they
swooped down on him, steered by their stiff, long tail-
feathers. The weeds in the ditch had hindered them
from pursuing their tactics, which were based on sudden
attack. But in the field they could resume their interrupted plan of campaign. One after the other they
swooped down and tore hair and bits of skin from him
with their beaks. Josse had numerous tears in his skin
and a big gash in one ear, and what was worse, his paws,
to his great surprise, became suddenly doubtful whether
they could give these crafty pursuers the slip.

In his doubt Josse stood still for a moment and rose
on his hind legs to look for a place of refuge. The magpies flew around him in close circles and came gradually
down to earth, in order to advance to the attack with
quick hops. He took the method that had helped him
before with the big dog. He bluffed—he fooled his pursuers; he snorted in their faces and scratched at them
with his claws. And to his great surprise it worked
immediately.

The magpies drew back and held council, debating as
to how they could carry on the attack. Could they have
been mistaken? Perhaps it wasn't a leveret at all, but a
rat, since he took such a fighting attitude?

The wafting spring wind that had been Josse's foster-
mother and, on the day when he had been born moist
and naked on the cold grass of the mound, had done her
best to dry him, was with him now; the magpies had to
turn and twist perpetually to keep their long tails out
of the wind. But the booty tempted them; even if he

was a sharp-toothed rat they would cripple him—yes, even if he was a kitten!

With a shrill screeching sound the cock magpie attacked him in front while the hen lurked behind. Then he set forward again in long, swift leaps, with the magpies' furious war-cry behind him.

But now something happened which neither Josse nor his pursuers had reckoned upon. On his way he fled across a meadow, and in the midst of this meadow there was a pond by which some lapwings dwelt.

He heard their cry of "Pee-wit!" from in front of him. Diving and soaring they flew quickly across the meadow. The birds were fuming with rage and their crests bristled each time they shrieked their cry: "Pee-wit, pee-wit!" Before poor Josse's eyes they gleamed black or white according to the way they turned their backs or underparts towards him. Now they were near. Josse perceived the flapping of their wings and the wind blustering and playing in their outstretched flight-feathers. He shivered. Yet more enemies had come against him.

But in this case the lapwings proved his friends. The magpies had recently emptied their nest of eggs; they had flown over the sprouting corn; the hen lapwing had been hatching, her breast closely covering her speckled eggs. They had found her out and driven her up. Fluttering awkwardly, one of the pies had kept the pair of lapwings in play, while the other had plundered the nest. The vengeful lapwings were now going resolutely for the magpies! Rising high, they rushed down upon them, coming blustering up on their broad, mobile wings, and flew shrieking across their path. With sudden downward darts and violent upward bursts they frisked about the egg-thieves, giving them enough to do.

Meanwhile little Josse showed a clean pair of heels. He hurried across the meadow, where the black shadows of the lapwings and magpies quite confused him, and found himself down in a ditch, then at a hawthorn bush, and under the tangle of its branches his ill-treated back came ruefully to itself. His eyes glowed, his flanks quivered . . . his resting paws were folded under him. In the distance he heard the incessant, high, intrepid war-cry of his rescuers: "Pee-wit, pee-wit!"

The passage with the magpies, thanks to the brave little hen lapwing, turned into an adventure which enriched Josse's experience.

Now he spent several nice, pleasant days, which passed smoothly without any disconcerting event. The wounds on his side and ear closed up and healed. He became so careful about exposing himself that in the dawn or twilight, when he grazed, he did so by stealth, with his neck between his shoulders and his ears flat. His senses were, so to speak, on tiptoe, always awake and perceptive, more particularly with regard to things that might come upon him from the air.

The grass became softer and more juicy. The fields grew green. The cock lapwing grew more silent. His mate was hatching for the third time.

Josse saw the larks, with their crests erect. They were about him for days on end. He saw them rise trilling jubilantly up towards the clouds, then fall down silently, like stones. They hid themselves from him, stealing away, bent forward through the grass, their crests always erect.

A lark would often hang low on quickly flapping wings, bent like the moon's sickle, directly over its tuft of grass, showing him its long fantail, with the two white rudder-feathers. It would sing to him and to the rye and the young clover.

Night after night brought new birds, with fine, gay summer colours. One noon a swift little flier awoke him, snatching at a fly over his head. "Twee-tweet-weet!" twittered the swallow, and Josse knew what it meant.

The cuckoo, too, the troll-bird of the Danish June, soon arrived. Shy and fidgety, it ran along fences and hedges, crying "Cuckoo, cuckoo!" or making a cracked sound as if it were just about to burst out laughing.

The nights were light and the air was warm, of course —life was as it should be!

Josse had now forsaken the lime pits and lived out in the open country in fields and meadows, in ditches and hedges. He had to have the sky all round him and about him—he had to see far—far!

One afternoon when he was sitting in a field near the lime pits in a strip of wheat along by the dike, he heard the wheat-ears whispering louder and louder. He raised himself up a little and scented—and saw. It was a dog a good way ahead.

His acquaintance with Kora had given him the opportunity of coming up against the scent of a dog. He was also strongly impressed by it. It was not quite so sharp and offensive as that of a fox, but on the other hand it was more full-bodied, greasy and nauseating. His delicate senses very quickly informed him that the bouquet that was on its way to him now was in no respect inferior to Kora's.

Tramp, tramp! Now he heard it. It was a ponderous, heavily moving cur with a mighty chest, wide mouth, and paws like the hooves of a horse.

It came lounging along by the fence, lowering its big

head to every tuft. Slowly and soberly moved the stiff legs, the feet planted deeply in the earth. If it had come quickly it would have startled Josse; but its low, tentative approach allayed his fear.

The dog went farther off, then came nearer. Still Josse took no notice. Then a big, dribbling mouth came panting down over his cover. Josse thought it had no business to do that. What did that big mouth want with such a tiny little thing as he?

To a hunting dog the discovery of Josse would have caused a slight shock to the nerves. Tramp took it with complete calm. He didn't know what nerves were! Josse was a rat, and rats are meant to be eaten. . . . Tramp's eyes became fierce. He opened his huge jaws. . . .

With an effort Josse shook his inertia from him, sprang at the beast's nose, and gave it a couple of sharp scratches.

But that wouldn't do this time! Tramp grabbed the tuft of grass with his teeth, tore it up and shook it. Josse only saved himself by a neat jump in the very nick of time.

That gave him a shock, but it taught him a lesson.

Since Tramp was half blind in one eye and the weeds grew high and thick by the fence, he slipped away unnoticed.

Tramp took his failure with the greatest equanimity. He was used to that kind of thing with rats. One couldn't catch them every time.

A week later another pair of jaws found Josse out, and from this pair came Reynard's acrid, repulsive scent. But now Josse had some experience on which to build. Fortunately for him he didn't try to bluff this time: he took to his heels in a trice and slipped away safely in the darkness, his back very wet.

What did he know now? He knew the caw of the crow, the blow of a magpie's wing, the scent of the dog —nay, even more: he knew that the greasy odour and the acrid smell were connected with jaws and white teeth.

The cows were out at grass, and to rest amid the clover's luxuriant tufts became more and more dangerous. With the cows came bellowing and clinking, men's speech and the rattling of pails. When the cows were milked, in the morning, at noon and in the evening, the house dogs came out, together with fat, milk-pampered cats.

The lapwings were quarrelsome; they thought no one else but themselves had any right to be in the fields. Even Josse they chased. He had just recently had a little adventure with them.

One morning he had been staying in the lime pits, and he and Lab had been out for a walk near the dancing-stone when the lapwings had come scurrying up with wings half raised like shields towards them. The gaiety and self-confidence had gone from their voices; instead, they gave forth long-drawn angry shrieks.

Josse paid no attention to the birds but began to graze along the edge of a pool.

It was boggy, miry and wet by the pool, but the grass was rich and delicate. A lump of clay suddenly excited his curiosity. It was warm, too; lumps of clay weren't usually warm! Now the lump rose up and revealed legs —legs that scampered over the muddy ground like the lapwing's. When he came near, the lapwing chicks became lumps of clay again.

Their mother wailed. But now the father came hurrying up. He made sharp, swooping dashes above Josse, shrieking his imperious "Pee-wit, pee-wit!" into his ear.

It was now above him, now before his nose. He heard the rustling of its feathers and the flapping of its wings, and he made haste to take cover.

Yes, the lapwings were quarrelsome; but in spite of that he soon learned to be on friendly terms with these ranters, and to turn their watchfulnes to good account. Night and day alike they were at their posts. They gave warning of cat, fox, dog, hawk—and man.

He could depend upon the lapwings when, tired and weary after his night's wandering, he lay down to rest and doze. They were his ubiquitous spies.

He had returned to Jens Tyrbag's fields. They were more luxuriant than others in the vicinity, and he was left somewhat more in peace there. He had for a long time been on good terms with Kora, who was Tyrbag's field dog. She hadn't the same fierce streak which was natural to Tramp. Josse was quite sure that he had nothing to fear from her.

Kora only moved as much as was absolutely necessary and, as the summer sun now warmed her coat, Josse scarcely met her in the fields at all. But he knew quite well where she was. She stayed amid a big pile of heavy, dark stones, the heap where she lived, a lair where she was protected from rain and wind. There she panted in the shade day after day.

The farmer's other dog undoubtedly interested Josse much more. It was mere vermin compared with Kora, but was of quite a different temperament. Fille was a female too—Jens Tyrbag could, generally speaking, scarcely endure anything masculine about him. She was an aggressive cur, with a sucking-pig's head, a fox's ears, four sticks of legs, and a tail like a post-horn. Her body was as plump as a sausage, for she was about to have pups.

Fille never appeared in the fields in the cold season, but lay at home on the sofa or slept in an old hay box by the warm kitchen range. Only when the air became summery and all that was damp and slushy had become firm and dry did she make up for this. She was no hound or game-finder of breeding, and definitely preferred to dig in a soft, light, accessible molehill to pricking her nose on a hedgehog that had rolled itself up into a ball. The little cur wasn't the least bit dangerous to Josse.

Josse had danced until the May sun had almost turned him from a humming-top into a clod. Then he fell asleep.

He slept, but not as men sleep, or as beasts of prey sleep, sunk in themselves. No, Josse slumbered as lightly as flowers and grass.

The next time lapwings awakened him, a sound for which his experience could give him no reason approached him quickly through the grass. He ducked down lower; but curiosity got the upper hand of him, and for a moment he raised his head carefully, his ears laid back.

It was Fille, with her fox-ears and stick-like legs. She stood a little way from him with staring eyes and one foreleg raised, her pointed, conical, rat-like muzzle quivering. It sank down into the clover—and now Josse saw that she was sniffing exactly at the path that he had trodden that morning. She had been taking a walk round and had now come by chance upon a big new molehill which rejoiced her. It seemed likely that she would find her way to his lair. She could find exactly each spot on the molehill where Josse had planted his feet.

Again he ventured to peep with one eye over the

tuft of grass and saw Fille trotting quickly along and sniffing loudly towards him. The conflict between his back and his paws began, and was so violent that his back quivered. But at last he decided to stay. His legs said: "Time enough yet!"

Fille went on and stopped by turns; she had not a hound's nose, hence she was often in doubt, and it didn't help matters when she tried a little détour.

She had to go back again to the molehill, where the scent now led her in quite another direction.

Fille sniffed and sniffed and set to work with her paws. Yes, no doubt, the little fellow was down there; as a rule one was more likely to come upon a mole under the earth than over it!

Then Josse's paws shrieked that now he should seize the opportunity to flee! His back protested quite positively, reminding him that it was daytime, of the light and the magpies; but the paws brought up Tramp's jaws and Reynard's snout. . . . In a twinkling Josse had come to the point when he had to decide to stay or to flee—and when it came to that, all his experience went for nothing.

But he didn't start off like a Jack-in-the-box, he didn't jump up crying: "Ho, ho, here am I!" No, his cunning had awakened, his little bit of a brain had come into play.

His ears were laid along his neck and his loins quivered while his paws stole like larks through the grass. They still itched to strike out in a run, but it was his back that had its way. Humped together, he moved along the earth until he was out of earshot, and then with a pattering of paws and a flapping of ears he was away.

First of all he chose his day-form in a delightful little

place between a couple of clods, where a great deal of seed had been spilt and where, therefore, the ears of spring-sown grain grew thickly. They were even more closely crowded together in a depression that Josse's back fitted very comfortably.

In half an hour Fille had levelled the molehill, but had made no discovery except that moles as a rule are not often to be found, even *under*ground! She trotted away and came straight to the place where Josse had lately lain. The form was still warm, and the pressed-down cushion of verdure showed the neatest impression of Josse's round hind quarters. Then the little cur yelped! To hunt by scent in the proper sense of the word was beyond her powers, but anyhow she could track a little. And now she started off, with her nose to the earth, through the clover. The only thing that stuck up was her post-horn of a tail.

Josse heard yelping; he sat up, following Fille's course anxiously with his eyes and ears. He noticed now that a dog can find anybody by his track. He saw Fille quickly approach the places where he had previously thought of lying. He had chosen his refuge carefully; he knew he had used every possible precautionary measure for concealing his track. He had hopped silently; he had never sat down—and yet a dog like Fille could follow his hidden path and was upon him, just as if he had been sitting still in one place. This was at that time completely incomprehensible to him.

But now his back had to go out into the fields—no help was to be had from dear mother earth. He ran with all his might, racing through the spring-sown corn, over pools—with yelping in his ears and a dog's panting breath behind him! Loose earth, scattered by his feet, flew into his ears. He came to a ditch and skipped across it, just as the dog was close upon his heels.

Then the yelping stopped all of a sudden; the pattering of paws could be heard no more, and the indefinite sense of danger was gone from the air. He slackened his pace and finally sat down. Then he raised himself high on his back legs and peeped backwards. Where was Fille?

Fille had gone head over heels into the ditch, and made a terrible fuss as she came out of the muddy water.

This kind of thing in connection with a ditch was extremely interesting to Josse. He observed something else too, not quite so important. It was becoming gradually clear to him that he left his scent behind him in his tracks. Hence afterwards he never ran straight to the place he intended to lie in. He first ran a little way past it, turned round and ran back again, made several loops and hopped to the side, and finally, with a big jump, reached the place where he wanted to stay. By this means he disappointed his enemy and assured himself of a good rest while that enemy was occupied with his loopings and jumps to one side—and meanwhile he could observe his adversary thoroughly.

That was what one might reasonably call cunning. Men called it instinct; Josse was quite sure that it was something more. It was the result of the conflict between his back and his legs, and the outcome of his natural intelligence.

Of course Josse didn't learn such things all at once. More pursuers than Fille drove them thoroughly into his head. But he gradually learned the art of self-defence and became an expert as he grew older.

But Fille had had a little exercise. She was tired out

after her excursion, which had ended so distressingly far beyond her usual boundaries.

What she had been running after she hadn't the least conception, so, when she had got dry and had recovered a little, she felt quite proud about what had taken place. For the first time in her life she had been fortunate enough to come upon a "mole." she preened herself; her currish cunning told her that she had had a rare piece of good luck. It wasn't every day that one could hunt a mole *above* ground!

So Fille magnified the occurrence into a great adventure.

CHAPTER III

GIRIK, THE PARTRIDGE

GIRIK, the partridge, loved the open fields and never went anywhere else.

Where the fields lay in hills and hollows, where the flowers of meadow and marsh covered the low-lying country, where hedge and fence alternated with ditch and dike, and willows, poplars and one storm-beaten blackthorn were the only trees that rose skywards,—there Girik and his family dwelt.

When twilight came and the dew fell after sunset, and the horizon, hidden behind the distant woods, glowed brightly, sending its fiery gleams through corn and clover; when hedgehogs in the hedges raised their snouts to the sky and snails in the ditches began to glide out,—Girik shrilled his strange assembly-call loudly and masterfully over the field.

"Tee-ee," he crowed. "Tee-ee! I am Girik. Come together, ye partridges, the night is at hand. Let us gather into a flock and keep warm!"

But when day dawned, and the first tinge of wild rose-pink showed on a little cloud on the eastern horizon, when snails crept home and hedgehogs in the hedges rolled themselves into balls, he crowed victoriously, greeting the sun.

"Tee-ee! Tee-ee! I am Girik, strong and pert after my night's rest. Follow me, partridges, I'll lead you to your breakfast in a wheat-field, to your dinner in the rye, to a sand-bath on the sunny slopes, and to refreshing drink from brook and spring. Tee-ee! Tee-ee!"

Girik's boastful speech was justified. He knew the fields, he knew the whole district. His realm extended from the river on the west to the white tower high on a hill on the east; to the north his frontiers touched the mound, and to the south he could fly all over the lime pits.

He came to the mound in the amber dawn of a showery April day. At this time of year there was continuous crowing on top of the round, rain-polished stone. Here he fought his spring battle with other cocks for the sake of a little grey hen with black spots. She stepped uneasily about the hill while they fought. She had a long neck and pale, gleaming eyes. Here on the moss-clad side of the mound where God made the weeds grow and raised His seeds despite the ant and the field-mouse, Girik had had many a day of furious battle with jealous old cocks, and thus had won his mate.

Along a path through the spring-sown corn came Josse. He had been out for his breakfast after a long night's tour of *his* kingdom. He advanced in little short hops, all with his senses on tiptoe. From time to time

"Here he fought his spring battle"

he stood still and rose up on his tail, lifted his ears and sniffed the air. He didn't venture to go on until his immediate neigbourhood had been thoroughly investigated.

On the top of a molehill on the dike stood Girik. Black wavy lines showed on the down on his neck, which was grey with dew. The red feathers on his shoulders, ribbed with gold like ripe wheat, gleamed twice as red as usual in the rising sun. On the watered silk of his breast there grew a sort of shield of splendidly gleaming feathers, which shone when he moved like a cluster of the wild-pink's rust-brown flowers.

Josse sat fascinated, following him with his eyes. He wasn't quite sure whether this individual might not be a new species of magpie. Should he hide himself or flee?

Girik hopped up on to the top of the molehill and raised himself on his toes. Standing thus he spread out his dock-red fantail and raised its splendid plumage towards the clouds. He puffed out his body under his little drooping wings and took a deep breath of air. Then with a mighty effort he shrilled out his masterful assembly-call right over Josse's head.

"Tee-ee!" he crowed. "I am Girik and you are a little hare that scarcely knows how to walk on his legs."

A quiver went through Josse. He recognized the voice, having heard it one evening in the lime pits. Girik repeated his call, as if to impress it upon him. "Tee-ee! Tee-ee! Tee-ee!"

The cuckoo in the willows sent a red-gold gleam from its eyes. It trailed its wing-tips along the branch and, taking a deep breath that swelled under its throat, it gave forth its "cuckoo," which echoed far over the hills. White, warm sunlight fell on the spring-sown corn. Full day had at last arrived.

Along the field path came a girl leading a nanny goat. Gradually, as she approached, Girik's neck sank into his body, his straight legs shortened, his loins went up and his tail went down. He became a part of the molehill.

Josse looked at Girik and involuntarily imitated him —not suddenly, but unnoticeably, slowly transforming himself until the farmer's daughter had passed by.

On days when the refuge amid the reeds and in the fields was deserted, Girik would go wild without warning. He would call his mate and, when they heard stealthy feet in the stubble, they would fly up into the air like migratory birds and hide themselves high up under the clouds, until at last they came to earth again among birches and grey willows in a far-off place in the river valley.

Josse heard Girik more and more frequently and came to know him quite as well as he had long known the lapwings and the larks.

Girik lived a decent family life in the meadows, and the time had come when he was most happy with his little mate. He strutted round and round her, stretched out his neck and looked inquisitively about him. His black-spotted hen pecked seeds and plucked delicate grass, sunned herself or ran about care-free, with in-drawn neck, after the flies and worms. She did herself really well. Girik scarcely preened himself at all and didn't think of resting. He watched over her and was always at his post with head erect.

When Josse was taking his supper, he would suddenly see Girik's hooked beak and red chin rise up over a stone or dike, while a little brownish-black, sharp-sighted eye regarded him fixedly and unblinkingly. Josse might believe himself alone in the clover, but all at once a clod of earth would rise up, legs would shoot out from under it, and neck would appear!

Girik!

There he would be again, erect and motionless, staring at him with round, inquiring eyes.

Another clod of earth lying close by Girik's side would, on the other hand, lie still. Not allowing herself to be in the least disturbed, Mrs. Girik would continue to enjoy herself. She would go on with her toilet, which she had commenced, in the warm, sun-dried sand, or would throw herself sideways and lie down to rest on one wing.

The two of them were always together. If *she* went down into a ditch to look for a worm, *he* remained up on the edge and stood and strutted with the feathers bristling on his neck.

Then for a time Josse lost sight of the partridges.

Girik had found a nesting place for himself and his little hen. It was down at the foot of a dike, between the field and the low, damp edge of the pond. There, when the exuberance of May made a green maze of grass-blades round the dandelions' butter-yellow corollas, Mrs. Girik began to lay her eggs.

She laid them in a heap, at the side of and over each other; and the heap grew and grew, another egg being added each day. The eggs were an earthy colour with a faint grass-green tint, so that they looked just like blades and stems of grass. Finally, the full clutch of eighteen eggs had been laid in a pile. There was a regular peak on the top.

When the last egg crowned the pile Girik had grown tired of his fierce scraping and crowing. From being an impetuous suitor he had become a faithful, industrious and attentive mate, whose sole object was the welfare of the nest. He, who had previously danced on the green turf, wet with April showers, crazy with the joy of battle, now bustled about full of solicitude and ready to defend his nest.

A desire to rest had come over him. The challenge had gone from his voice. He crowed no longer but clucked softly. As far as he was concerned there was nothing in the fields except the nest.

On the dike stood posts holding up the wires of the fence round the pond. Inside as well as outside this fence heifers and colts came to graze. They stretched their munching mouths over and between the wires and browsed on the dike. So Girik had new enemies to deal with! But he showed them a brave front. No heifer or colt could put a muzzle near the tuft that hid the nest without Girik flapping and scratching, shrilling tumultuously and flying up at it.

One morning Josse came hopping along the dike, cheerful and full of vim as usual. He had made a discovery which was of immense importance to him. Out in the fields, at the end of a boundary fence, he had found an almost overgrown plot of land. It was an old holding, with a lot of brushwood and blackthorn round about it. Here no man interfered and no dog intruded. If he was in mortal danger here was a refuge where he could safely regain his breath and have a good rest. Somehow he felt that curiosity would not leave him in peace until, at the first opportunity, he had thoroughly explored his latest discovery. The weather was lovely; the sky was filled with floating, feathery clouds; the air was warm and pleasant.

He was passing by a willow when Girik suddenly darted up out of a tuft of grass.

He was all fire and flame. His feathers bristled, his

head was held erect. He had been lucky enough the day before to kill a mouse that had been passing by; and a grass snake, which probably hadn't had any evil intentions, he had disposed of that very morning. Now it was Josse's turn, the turn of that silly, long-legged creature who, with his senseless caperings, might easily disturb the calm of his beloved nest.

Girik went for Josse's head, crowing loudly, and attacking him simultaneously with claws and wings. When Josse turned back hastily, he got in a peck that plucked a big tuft of fur from Josse's hind quarters. Josse slipped into a little ditch, then into the corn, and ran from the place. He was upset over the encounter with Girik for the rest of the day.

A few days before it had been the lapwings, and now Girik—he had to be on the run the whole time!

There were many weeks of drought and of warm, lovely weather. He, who ordinarily didn't want to drink, grew quite thirsty on these long, warm days. He longed for evening's cool breeze and for the dewdrops that made everything so moist and fresh.

One afternoon he felt particularly like this. Left alone by Hopsy, he sat on the edge of the clover. Its forest of stems protected him from the heat. He could actually smell the heat in the leaden-blue, hazy air. It vibrated before his eyes; it contracted his nostrils. He was uneasy and couldn't sleep. The air grew hotter and hotter with every breath he took.

Clouds piled up on the horizon. A dirty-black bank of cloud rolled up and spread itself over Girik's realm. For the moment all colours showed clear and pure. The green earth was clothed in its very greenest garb, the lapwing's wings glistened snow-white, and Jens Tyrbag's dirty, yellow, farm buildings shone as if they had been newly painted. The sky grew blacker and blacker and great waves of wind swept the rye.

Larks dropped down on all sides of him. Swarms of flies made for their haunts. Tethered horses and cows ran round and round, and out of the corn Girik came hurrying, just as the first heavy drops fell. He ran out into the middle of the field path and peeped inquisitively upwards, his head aslant. Was it only dew or was it rain? The drops became big and one followed fast upon another. It grew lighter, but the horizon became like a grey wall. Girik took cover under a big burdock. He thought only of the nest, of the eggs, of his mate. But Josse humped his back; it was coming, he saw it— he had long felt it in the air.

When the lighting first lit up his shelter amid the clover, he started and trembled where he sat. His long ears dangled straight down on his neck and—oh, for shame!—his feet almost ran away with him.

The thunderstorm broke; Josse had his May-day baptism. He gave up trying to lick his paws dry: he was lucky if he could even shelter his body. Drop after drop fell from his fur, so that there was a big puddle under him and he had to change his place every minute. But only behind his ears did he *feel* at all wet, and that refreshed him.

The drumming of the warm, soft rain on the leaves stopped. . . .

A lark rose twittering and the oppression was lifted from Josse's breast. He peeped upwards and saw a bit of blue sky; the black clouds were far away behind the hill with the white tower. Everything about him was wet, but the cornfields smelt lovely, the rain had washed their fine, volatile scent down to the very earth. Swarms of flies were dancing over the corn again.

Josse just had to go out and take the air, so he set forth hopping into the grain and stuffed himself with the young, fresh oats. Here the wind and the sunlight dried his coat.

How well he slept there in the fields and how he grew as he slept!

CHAPTER IV

HOPSY AND LAB

SHE was called Hopsy be-
cause there was so
much kick and
spring in her paws.
She had never
tried the usual
hare's hop, which
begins suddenly
without a preliminary run by the springy strength of
the hind legs alone. It starts straight up from a sitting
position and ends somewhere out in the fields. She
couldn't manage that sort of thing, but she didn't particularly need to. She kept to little hops, and so she was
called Hopsy.

A shy and timid little thing was Hopsy. In all her
ways she gave an impression of complete defencelessness. She never came out of her tuft of grass in the daytime. It was only when the earth was wrapped in twilight
that she stole forth and began her nightly excursions.
But she seldom went far. As soon as she had her meal
she hid herself again.

She was always in doubt as to where she should lie.
When her stomach was full and her eyes dull she felt

a certain dislike of all white, red and yellow flowers, and preferred the less variegated flat places, feeling attracted by grey bark, brown soil and withered grass.

She was as matter-of-fact and thoughtful as Josse was frivolous, high-spirited and merry, and she very rarely allowed herself to be lured into taking part in his wild, careless gambols. *She* wouldn't be drawn into any of his imprudences out of sheer playfulness.

The essential differences between the characters of Josse and Hopsy had thus early made themselves evident. With Josse the paws had the last word, they wanted to go out and hop. He was never still. But with Hopsy it was the back that settled the matter. It pleaded its defencelessness and wanted to make the most of shelter; it forced the paws to keep quiet. Hence she avoided both magpie and fox; a dog scarcely ever found out her tuft. As soon as she noticed any rustling in her neighbourhood she sat motionless, and made herself so tiny that only by the barest chance could she be found.

Hopsy surrendered herself blindly and completely to the earth on which she was set.

Volatile Josse didn't recognize the necessity for this. It would only be impressed upon him by dearly-bought experience.

But on the whole he was more awake. He had become familiar with the world, and had acquired the ability to act thoughtfully. He had gained courage too—not the foolhardy, self-sacrificing courage that female animals had when they were looking after their young. No, it was the courage to save *himself* when the pinch came and he was in mortal danger.

Josse had to win experience, to live his life out to the last possible moment, and he would neglect nothing which helped him to do so. That was his nature, for he was a buck hare.

Lab was quite distinctly a little buck hare too, but he was denser; not nearly so alert and quick-witted. His name he owed to his paws, which were large and flat; they were set on the end of his rather long, thin legs like scrubbing-brushes on their handles, and when he was leaping about they smacked the earth hard and heavily.

The instinct to make the most of every means of defence that was born in his sister was also his to a certain extent. But there was no sympathy between his paws and his back. He hadn't Josse's speed or decision, or his fine, sharp perceptive powers. Nor was he able to determine when he should stay still and when he should flee. He often missed the happy moment when luck was on his side. If the fields had held as many foxes as they did dogs, he would have been done for long ago. And if he had had an adventure with the magpies it wouldn't have ended in a mere fright. But he was still alive, chiefly because fate had been so extremely kind to him as never to let him be really tested. He went on through life without having much opportunity to win experience: by day he slept, and at night his stomach was his chief concern. He had none of Josse's many and various adventures, but just knew the direction of the hedges and ditches and where the paths crossed in the fields he lived in.

Lab and Hopsy lay hidden in Jens Tyrbag's spring-sown corn or clover for days on end.

Josse met them more and more rarely, but from time to time they saw each other when he wanted to revisit his native lime pits. Josse cheered them up, infected them with his joy of life, and they all three took a pleasant hop together over the even country which the cows had cropped. They found several dancing-stones there, or loose molehills, on which it was amusing to scrape with eager toes.

Jens Tyrbag, who liked to exercise his horses himself in the early dawn, was diverted time and again by the three little creatures. He took special note of the smallest of them—if that fellow was in a bad temper, he thought or didn't like his food, he would be able to give some-one a good box on the ear!

He was thinking of those big feet, the only things which distinguished Lab from his brother and sister. Lab looked as if he had inherited his father's churlish disposition to a high degree! Unfortunately for his chance of survival this warlike appearance was of no particular use to him. On the other hand it was not without a certain significance in his life.

As the summer advanced, the leverets gradually be-came familiar with Farmer Tyrbag; they discovered that he could hear at about the same distance as cows and horses. From their refuge in his fields they made many observations; they learned to recognize the stroke of the mallet that drove in the tethering pegs, the rattling of the milk pails, and the merry milkmaid's shrill, discor-dant song. They learned to know men's trampling feet and the different tones of a dog's bark. Hopsy slept soundly; she left all the sounds about her go in at one ear and out at the other; she gadded about but little, it was true, yet she might have had plenty of experiences where she was, if she had only understood more of the world's strange and various tongues.

Josse was never quite sure that he had really been asleep! All the sounds he knew spoke to him, and with those that he didn't know he felt a strange urge to get better acquainted. But fortunately in the daytime he was now able to restrain himself.

Lab neither slept when he slept nor was he properly awake when he was awake; in a word, he always felt dull and sleepy. But in spite of that he wasn't devoid of understanding of what was going on around him. He had, besides his warlike appearance, a couple of other defects: he snored, and he didn't know it!

One summer night the moon rode white and round, but the sky was becoming blue and the earth was emerging from twilight. Time was moving on towards dawn.

Josse was in a good humour. He had been down in the lime pits and had made merry with his brother and sister and now he was coming along a dike between corn land and fallow land with Lab at his heels.

There was an old building at the end of the dike. It had once been a house with windows and chimneys, a home for a pair of humans; but now it was a ruin.

The garden hedge with its blackthorns and wild flowers, elders and lilacs and bird-cherry trees, still remained, but the garden itself was filled with weeds: mugwort, nettles and grass had overgrown it.

Here the farmer had piled up in a heap all the big stones which he had dug out of his fields. All kinds of other lumber was scattered round about it; rusty iron plates from kitchen ranges, saucepans with holes in them, and a very old-fashioned plough. Hops decorated the lumber as best they could and bindweed covered it with its green lacework, while cornflowers and poppies rivalled one another as to which could cover most ground with their coloured carpet.

The old house was indeed a shelter in the midst of the open fields; but it was well to be careful among the stones and the rubbish heaps outside. There dwelt Jit-Jit, the murderous weasel.

There was a burdock in the garden between the mug-wort and the grass. Its stiff, red-striped stem reared itself like a flagstaff high over the elders. Its topmost spike was rounded off with a bud. The bud was the beginning of the giant plant's flower. But its huge, flat leaves kept other plants from living near it, and gave shade to its roots so that they could survive the drought.

But Lab remained under the burdock. He was now tired and sleepy, and the burdock apparently offered him the most friendly shelter. Under there he was pro-tected from rain, which he avoided like the plague, and from crows, with which he had had his one and only adventure; so he made himself comfortable and was soon yawning.

Jit-Jit was out on her early morning hunt, with a zeal and a speed which one only meets in practised, highly-trained workers. Every movement was noiseless. Only now and then did she allow herself to look about and then it was always from a place where she had taken cover. Her long body, when she moved at full speed, was like a streak shooting through the grass, and when, with her fiery red fur, she crossed the top of a molehill, it seemed as if a sunray had shot across it. Jit-Jit's tactics were like those of a falcon. Her aim was sudden, her spring like lightning. There was no con-sideration, no mercy for her victim.

She seldom came out in the daytime, but in the twi-light of morn and eve. She was extraordinarily strong for her size and full of courage and the lust for murder. A little while ago she had had young, and as the fox, her great rival, was taking everything, times were bad.

For the fourth time that early morning she was on her way home with food.

When she heard Lab's monotonous, sonorous snoring, she stopped with a jerk. With the front part of her body lifted and with eagerly spying eyes she crept from her place through the elders and in under the burdock. A dry stick in the brushwood cracked beneath her. Lab awoke and, seeing he was in an advantageous position, determined not to stir from the spot.

Jit-Jit gave him no further time to consider; she sprang on him. He scarcely knew it when all was over. Deep in Jit-Jit's consciousness lurked a suspicion that at the moment when she sprang she had seen another leveret flash by like lightning. She must have that one too! With noiseless leaps she set forward in the direction it had taken.

Josse was inside the house looking round.

It was the greatest of joys to him when his eager feet passed over heap after heap of big, angular stones—the very kind his agile legs would fain have danced upon—and over many interwoven winding paths, which he must remember in case he had to dodge an enemy. Finally from a bed of nettles he caught sight of a delightfully smelling, spicy bit of green stuff, which his voracious teeth began to gnaw with the greatest eagerness.

The little bit of green was the old garden's last remnant of culture—an obstinate bit of parsley.

He was still at the height of his enjoyment when, for the first time in his life, he heard a hoarse sound. He listened with strained attention, but couldn't find out what it was. He started off to satisfy his curiosity and saw a long, yellowish-red, strange, softly moving little

animal coming to meet him. His mistrust at last awakened, and with the greatest possible speed he took cover
in a tuft of grass.

Jit-Jit came up and went round and round the tuft of
grass. This was done with a set purpose. By this means
she confused her inexperienced victim. Josse couldn't
find out whence the danger threatened.

When he was quite tired out, the grass tuft divided
suddenly. With all her might Jit-Jit sprang at his neck.
But she was in too great a hurry. She didn't get hold
of the skin, nor did she manage to fasten her teeth into
her prey. Josse darted forward with gigantic hops, his
feet rushing over the ground, farther, farther, while Jit-
Jit, half-riding, half-running, rushed forward along with
him. Josse shrieked, but without hearing his own voice.
All he was conscious of in that moment of mortal danger
was the blackthorn bush in the garden hedge.

The very night before he had discovered this blackthorn bush, and it had had a message for him. Now he
cast himself into it, seeking the promised salvation.

And the blackthorn bush didn't fail little Josse. As,
wild with fear, he rushed into the midst of its thorny
branches they pressed his vile rider so sharply that the
weasel was torn completely off, turning a somersault
right over the garden fence.

At that very moment an old vixen with alert, pricked-
up ears popped out on the other side. Amazement
mingled with joy gleamed in her cunning eyes. Perhaps
she could bring off a coup here! Tired of nursing her
cubs, she had been lying sound asleep on a heap of hay
when the pitiful shrieks of the dying Lab had awakened
her fully to life. She had sprung up and listened atten-
tively. In a few moments Josse's shrieks had followed,

and now she stood there with her questing nose right in front of the confused Jit-Jit.

But the daring little weasel didn't allow herself to be confused. She stared the vixen steadily in the eyes. The sight of her big rival and hereditary enemy increased her desire for prey and her lust for murder. She had fortunately defeated her first victim, tasted the first warm drops of its blood, and now—now—came this fox, who might deprive her of the chance of conquering the other too.

The vixen was surprised. Her joyful hope that alone and in the deepest quiet she might be able to help some poor hare over a little difficulty in the hedge had ended in smoke with this unexpected meeting. But she couldn't imagine whence came the hare's shriek—she didn't *see* any hare.

The weasel had no mind to explain to the vixen the misfortune which had overtaken her. She prepared for action; she sat half erect with glittering eyes and eager teeth. The sly creature was meditating evil under her fiery, yellow coat which now shone violet and gold in the rays of the rising sun. A few moments passed in strained expectancy.

It was that rapacity and that boldness which finally decided her mode of procedure. The stiff-eared fox, not content with depriving her of her prey, might invade her dwelling and perhaps make a breakfast off her young ones.

Her awakened mother-instinct and her measureless greed for prey were closely allied. She would kill the vixen as she would kill a badger! Like a sudden flame she shot up out of the grass.

She fastened on the vixen's tenderest place; on the black cartilage of her nose! Now she had the whip-hand, even though the vixen was so much larger than herself, just as a herd-boy has control of a bull with a ring in its nose. The vixen snorted and hissed. She stood with pitifully humped back and tail between her legs, unable to move.

Jit-Jit's littles eyes glowed with savagery and greed like live coals. She uttered a series of short, piercing squeals and, standing on her hind legs, began walking backwards, hauling the vixen along. But close by there was a little water-hole which a thunder shower had filled to the brim.

A gleam of hope and joy at Jit-Jit's coming misfortune came into the tortured vixen's desperate eyes, as she saw that chance was lending her a helping hand.

With an effort she took two, three, long jumps forward, and swung the weasel like a proboscis before her into the air. Then she plunged her foolhardy little enemy into the muddy water.

But Jit-Jit held on fast.

Now the question was which could hold its breath the longest.

Time after time the vixen ducked her head almost down to the bottom of the mud-hole without the clutch on her muzzle loosening in the least. The water cooled the cunning fox's muzzle and calmed her pain as she dragged her aggressive, foolhardy little assailant round in the mud so much that the weasel got its mouth full and had to let go at last.

The fight had gone out of both duellists!

Jit-Jit disappeared into the grass; she would have quite enough to do for the time being to lick herself dry and clean. The fox, too, thought it advisable to move on. With what felt like a gadfly stinging the end of her nose, she slunk off into a patch of corn.

Meanwhile Josse got off lightly. While his malicious persecutors, yellow with envy and considerably mishandled, slunk away, he took to his heels and ran back along the boundary dike and into the clover, where sensible Hopsy had long ago retired to rest.

The heat quivered in the clover where Hopsy lay. She had found a little hollow, deep down at the bottom of the forest of leaves. Over her waved the summer wind and a wood of heart-shaped leaves. An immense bumble-bee had been buzzing about in the fields the whole morning. Sometimes it was just in front of her and sometimes a good distance away. The bumble-bee was questing through the field as all bumble-bees do.

There it was again! Hopsy distinctly heard its monotonous hum and the rustle of its wings.

There was something suspicious about the insect! The nearer it came to her the more certainly her ears knew that they had been mistaken. No, that was no bumble-bee! Now it became clear to her that it was a beetle, a big, clumsy beetle that crawled about and scolded in a discontented tone between its vain attempts to fly upwards.

The beetle was really a mowing-machine rolling round the clover-field. Its worn cog-wheels smacked their broad teeth hard and ferociously against each other; axles hummed, cranks hammered, and the sharp-bladed knives rattled and cut. The sweeping scythes cut the grass right at the roots. If a sitting partridge or a bewildered and defenceless little hare got into their power, they cut them to bits.

Nearer and nearer to Hopsy the machine ate its way. Hopsy had already been exposed to many dangers and had come out of them safely by merely sitting still. She relied upon the earth. She kept still. The fox might sneak by a foot's breadth from her tuft—she kept still. The dog that went about in the fields might, as it went, brush the fur on her back with its foreleg; she pressed closer to the earth. A cat might sit in the grass before her and listen to what was going on in the fields about it—the tip of its tail might curl over the back of her neck and tickle her on her sensitive muzzle—it didn't affect her. She still remained crouching and making herself as flat as possible.

The machine had gone nearlly all round the field. Now Hopsy lay directly in its path. Already she felt the earth shaking under hoof-beats. But she knew them; they didn't frighten her. A moment later the knives were clattering just behind her back.

In her shelter it grew lighter and lighter. The soft, shadowy tints changed, and grey moths and many-coloured little butterflies fluttered away. The long, swaying rye-grass that was among the clover-stems stood for a moment dancing over the cutting knife-edge. Then it wavered and reeled heavily over to rest in a heap. The roof, in fact the whole house, was falling over Hopsy. But she let it fall! With her whole body from head to tail pressed close to the earth and her eyes bulging half out of their sockets, she pressed herself down into her little hollow. And the hollow saved her. The rolling guillotine with its cruel clattering passed over her back.

It was now open and sunny about her. She waited for a moment thinking that the wind would blow the clover erect again. Finally she got up and started off into a neighbouring patch of rye.

Josse too sat in the clover-field—and how did *he* manage?

He managed magnificently. He was too volatile to get into Hopsy's situation. His trust in the earth didn't hold. He had stopped going into deep clover. It was too tall for him, too thick and too dark. He kept to the outer edge.

As soon as the machine began its first round he knew at once that it was no bumble-bee or beetle, but more like a nasty, ferocious dog. So he decamped. With light, elastic leaps and quivering loins, and his ears laid along his back, he ran to the field path and then into a deep ditch which he knew. Now in the middle of the day, when the sun blazed, everything was so hazy and misty to him that he had to keep along the edge of the ditch in order to find his way. Without any more trouble than when he was closely pursued by the lapwings, he climbed out of the ditch and hid himself in a tuft of rushes on a peninsula in the pond.

He had made great discoveries that day; he had discovered a new "dog," a whole heap of dancing-stones, and the parsley—and he had discovered something else too—the weasel!

CHAPTER V

AT THE POND

THE pond was situated in the outer fields in a hollow between the hillocks. Reeds and rushes lined its edges and here and there on bumps of higher ground about it, sedge shot up thickly. In places milfoil covered the water with its thick, tough growth. A few small poplars and willows stood near the path trodden by the animals coming to drink. Sheep and colts had gnawed their bark and heifers and bullocks had torn the wood with their horns.

Meadow-flowers, in all their midsummer loveliness, massed round the pond. Between heart-grass and valerian, coarse cabbage-thistles lifted their heads into the air and in damp, level places floated fan-like tufts of sweet-grass. On marshy ground irises were enthroned and bulrushes showed their heads, while along the furrows that bounded this little wilderness on every side corn-mint crept luxuriantly over the dark, heavy clay.

The mint was a feature of the place. In big, bushy clumps it swelled over the clods and filled the air over the pond with its sweet perfume. Together with the scent of ripe fruit and of the meadows in the sun, of the thunder-shower's warm, refreshing drops, came that of the wild parsley with its widely-branching stems. The moorland women came here to gather this spicy herb, which grew almost on their thresholds.

This pond was the only one in the village. It had a voice. The water had tongues. It was trilling loudly now. The trilling became clearer and stronger, it lured him to it and led him on. There is nothing so lulling and enticing as the trilling that bubbles up from the water round the edge of a pond. It came from the hill's native toads.

He was out on one of the enclosed fields near the village pond when he first saw calves. They were very small and were lying down. A delightful plant, the pink, grew wild here, having seeded from the gardens, and rose up in the grass among the little creatures. For a long time Josse had sniffed its fine, spicy smell in his nose. Now he fell upon it.

The pink is a great delicacy. But as he sat and munched he suddenly felt a rough, moist muzzle touching his. A new-born calf which lay tethered there had mistaken, in its ignorance, Josse's warm nose for its anxiously-awaited mother. Josse thought that perhaps the muzzle was out for the pinks and gobbled them still more eagerly. Then he noticed something that was cautiously trying to grip one of his ears. The little calf thought delightedly that at last it had got hold of its mother!

It was just one of those things which might occur in the fields and which had no longer any power to

frighten Josse. He just drew his ear back and smacked
the calf on the nose with his paw; then he snatched up
the rest of the pinks in one mouthful and hopped out
of range of the animal. The calf turned its head away
despondently and again fell into a deep sleep.

Josse had begun to value this pleasant pond. It had
been one of his first discoveries when he had left the
lime pits behind him for good. When flocks of wild
ducks stood in the water in the late twilight he often
came down to gnaw a little at aspen and willow and to
smell the mint. And when men wearied him with their
noisy behaviour, he used to steal away from the day's
noises and come here where the land moved its foot as
far forward as possible into the water. Here he enjoyed
his sleep, well hidden in a tuft of sedge, warmed by the
sun and lulled by the pleasant lapping of the ripples.
Here, in the corn-mint's kingdom, the other side of his
nature, the reflective, philosophical side, had quiet to
develop.

Very little ever happened here by the pond.

Sometimes the lambs, taking a little stroll, would sniff
near him. Then he snorted and reared. Fille sometimes
appeared hunting round after lapwings. Then Josse
made off. He knew her and knew that with a few
tricks and a little guile he could get the better of her.
One day the farmer's little cur pursued him so hard that
he couldn't get away. He grew so frightened that, without thinking what he was doing, and just following his
nose, he went head over heels into the water.

The water was rather nasty and very wet. Josse knew
that; but he had no choice: he had to hurry.

Fille knew it too and sat howling on dry land.

From time to time the magpies, who had just hatched
out their young, flew over the pond looking for snail-

shells on its banks. Josse was still a desirable tit-bit for them. Big gulls on still wings and swift hawks with greedy, spying eyes flew from time to time quite close to his tuft; but none saw him and none found him. He knew how to hide himself really well.

It happened one afternoon that a big, blue-backed bird with the sunny gleam of the ripples on its breast flashed like lightning over the pond, unannounced by the lapwings. Rising suddenly, turning sharply and shrieking as it swooped, the falcon hunted an unfortunate, hoarsely quacking wild duck.

The duck's two little downy ducklings sought refuge and cover right in Josse's tuft while their parent risked her life for them. When she saw that they were safe she dived into the water and escaped from the falcon. But Josse was alarmed and his little heart beat fast. For this once he let in the uninvited broad-beaked little creatures. But he wanted peace and quiet in his tuft and snorted at the mother duck when she came up with her ducklings.

It was in the night that Josse got into his swing and gave his soft, furry paws free play. From early evening until early dawn he raced about, listened, and smelt. At the least suspicious sound he at once put on speed and made himself invisible in no time. Night after night he charted his country; his long black legs were his compasses; with their help and that of his delicate senses he got well acquainted with hedge and ditch, pond and boundary.

He went thoroughly to work and wasn't content with just noting where a hedge began and where a ditch flowed out. No, he had to know every bit of the way; he had to put his nose on each stone, each tuft; he had to set his paws on every square foot of earth.

He had to know his whole little kingdom, down to the smallest details. There was one thing which had peculiar significance—the location of human habitations and their relation to boundaries and fields and to one another; also gaps in the hedges, fords over ditches, and bridges over brooks and rivers. Men's roads and paths mustn't be forgotten. He went over them all and measured them thoroughly, keeping records in his brain of the measurements.

Hopsy only knew Jens Tyrbag's fields; Josse soon knew most of the parish.

Dikes and ditches were Josse's roads, but he ran neither right on the top nor at the bottom—just along by them. He was well acquainted with the fact that in their undergrowth lurked the fox and the weasel. In spite of that he knew how to make use of them. They led him surely along in his nightly excursions round the hill with the white tower on top, and up and down among the many scattered settlers' farms. In each farm lived a dog —and in Bjaerg village there lived many. At night he often sat for a long time listening to the different barks that marked the various dogs' modes of life and temperament. He knew where each one lived. But of them all he was only constantly in touch with Tramp, Kora and Fille.

Among the unknown barks he noticed one particularly. It had a peculiar, shrill, hateful, angry tone; it never moved from place to place on the farm as the others did, but always remained at one and the same spot.

It was a watch-dog in a stone heap that lay by itself a little way from the hill. In the fields he had nothing to fear from this dog as he sat and looked about him.

Josse had to make a big détour every night, for he

was obliged to have strong and varied nourishment, and required a variety of plants. Many were purely medicinal, for use against the diseases with which he had to reckon as enemies. He was very dainty and ate only the most delicate blades of grass or corn, so that the corn and grass grew the more quickly for his nibbling.

He ate in the greatest haste. He moved in brisk, energetic hops from place to place in the grass, rapidly found the plants he wanted, cropped a mouthful in three or four bites, threw his ears back and set his nose to the wind while he chewed and munched.

If there came a loud barking from a farm, or if there was shouting and noise, he at once raised his long nose into the air for a moment and his jaws ceased to move as he turned his ears in the direction from which the noise came and listened.

He needed only a second of strained attention to be clear about the nature of the disturbance—to know whether it was serious for him, whether it might bring him danger . . . then he lay his long, betraying ears down on his neck and filled his mouth again.

The important thing was that his senses should always react to his surroundings.

When he was full, he went on making a thorough reconnaissance at every third or fourth hop. He stopped on the tops of hillocks and at crossways, sitting there a long time, raised on his hind legs with staring eyes and sharp ears looking at and listening to the countryside and his nose inquiringly sniffing the air.

A white cat with a black tip to its tail glided like a shooting star over the flat, fallow land in the gathering darkness. It disappeared suddenly into the wheat.

From the stone heaps humans set up a din of gramophones and concertinas in rivalry with one another. But out where Josse was on top of the parish dike only the evening twittering of the swallows, the crowing of the little partridge, and the far-off cuckoo's call could be heard.

There he sat with his short forelegs resting lightly on the ground ready to make himself invisible with one spring. His erect ears straggled a little, like funnels sticking out on each side. Thus he communed with the world and in quiet and peace made his profound observations. His nose in the middle of his muzzle quivered at every sound. It moved round in the air, his whiskers bristling when the baying of dogs died in the distance and the carts rolled away; approaching sounds caused both muzzle and ears to droop.

Darker and darker grew the night about him. Beetles sat with their buzzers pointing upwards and from corn and clover came white, noiseless ghost-moths that sailed up into the air and let themselves be borne far, far away. A cool breeze stirred Josse's whiskers.

Now the gramophones were silent. It grew quiet in the village on the hill. The gardens enclosed the white-washed farmhouses and darkness enclosed the white tower. Josse heard people come out and listen and say good-night to the earth.

In the thick foliage of the pea-fields, where by day toads and frogs hid deep down from the storks, his teeth luxuriated in the long pods. He was happy, so happy.

Josse was satiated. Along an enchanted path amid the corn he came, cheerfully hopping with all the mid-summer night in his blood, and began to race along the wheel-tracks. Before he knew it he was out at the end of the fence. The path turned sharply towards the hill. Curiosity seized him.

It had driven him to the first roller, the first harrow,

the first plough that had lain in the fields. Thoughtfully he set himself to the task of exploring the place where dwelt all the sounds of the daytime.

The village was dead, silent and still as it always was at night. Broad and open lay the rough, sun-baked road. He could follow it where it ran between the gardens in which flowering elders gleamed. The road took a turn. Whither did it lead? Josse was filled with the desire to find out.

With his heart jumping about in his body in competition with his feet, he let himself be drawn onwards. Fear rode behind him, but curiosity was at work in his back legs . . . he must go on . . . on!

This was his first real trip abroad into the strange and the unknown.

The great stone heap on the hill shone among the bushes and trees. He smelt a well-known smell which he remembered from the field, manure heaps. The big stone heaps encircled an open space in the middle. Here it was flat and roomy. He might try a few dance-steps. The scent of parsley came to him in thick clouds from the gardens as he ran along under the quickset hedges. There were many other spicy plants too, he saw.

All the gates and shutters stood wide open; the light night wandered unhindered in and out. Josse observed that the stone heaps consisted of lesser stone heaps, among which men had their paths and different openings, just as the weasel in the hedge had his. He followed the broadest of the paths, which ended in a big opening in the middle of one of the stone heaps and the big gate which stood right in front of it.

A draught of nauseating, heavy air met him, and brought his little feet to a full stop. He smelt dog, cat, cow, and horse. For a long time he sat and listened.

Dull, subdued waves of snoring came through the little apertures in the stone heap, together with the other natural sounds of cattle and humans who hold converse with life in their sleep. But at length prudence got the upper hand of curiosity. He knew that it was better for him to make off.

He followed the man-track between the stone heaps a little further, and each time that he sat down and listened and considered he noticed a new, delicious, spicy perfume: he smelt thyme, cabbage, and fruit-tree bark . . . things which made his mouth water.

Suddenly there came a pitiful screaming on one of the manure heaps. The cries turned to snorts and hisses. Then the yard dog took it upon himself to establish order and the peace of the night. He scolded the cats—the cats scolded back at him. Josse streaked back at full speed across the open space where the pond lay and out again into the fields.

He was a little flurried, but delighted, for he had had a great experience. He had been right up into the village on the hill!

CHAPTER VI

DANGER!

AT THE extreme end of the village on the hill dwelt Tramp, like a big tiger.

He had a mania for scaring horses. He lay in ambush in the ditches, by the wayside or behind a garden hedge, and would suddenly break out with bristling mane and a threatening bark. He was also the kind of dog that rushes at cyclists. When a cycle approached his farm he put his tail down and stood meditatively and indifferently staring at the turn of the road—but at the very moment when the unsuspecting cyclist was right in front of him he swerved round and made for him with a fierce bellow. If the cyclist dismounted, he was afraid and made tracks for his farmyard.

He was a hater of everything that went on wheels; only milk-carts were in harmony with his evil, treacherous mind. If a milk-cart drove into the farmyard, he jumped round it on his hind legs; and set up a wild war-dance.

Josse could hear him where he sat looking out ovei the country. Tramp's dry, hollow, booming thunderclap of a voice was heard all over the parish!

He only followed people into the fields when the weather was fine. He never went further than to the actual spot where work was to be done, and there he stopped with drooping head and gaping jaws and his long, red tongue hanging out of his mouth. He might stay for half an hour dozing there, while the cowman milked or herded the cattle together.

His specialty was rats. This weakness and his idiotic hatred for everything that moved quickly had Josse's full attention. Josse knew him inside out and was quite well aware that it was this big bellowing fellow that had recently had him in his jaws.

But there was another dog which had begun to attract Josse's interest to a considerably higher degree. This personage was Kasper—a long-legged cur with a black cut-away chest and a high, shrill voice.

Kasper's coat was hay-colour. Right from his nose to the tip of his tail, on back and belly, nay, even on the under-side of his thighs, his coat was of the same melancholy, monotonous hue. The dog was like a living bit of his farmstead's faint ochre-yellow buildings.

There were two natures in Kasper. His mother had been a watch-dog of the Bromhold race, his father a thoroughbred retriever who would have been glad of a chance to taste poultry or lambs. Kasper had his mother's skin, her long, hanging, strangely square ears and mild, dreamy eyes. He had, too, a share of her temperament. For instance, when out walking he would stand still for a long time, sink his head deeper and deeper towards the earth, till finally he fell asleep. He could sleep both standing and walking.

But when darkness fell he took on his father's nature and became lively and fierce. Josse always heard him come out of the gate and begin to bark. At night he slunk about the whole time, now in the farmyard, now in the garden. He never touched rats; it seemed as though he knew that it would be impossible to keep the farm-yard free of them. But foxes and weasels that wanted to get at the poultry, and hares that wanted to get at the cabbages, he couldn't endure; as soon as ever his nose gave him notice of their noiseless approach he started off and frightened them away. At midnight when the moon was full his coat turned chalk-white. It made Josse shiver when he came too near the farm and suddenly caught sight of the pale watcher. There stood Kasper, turned as it were to stone, in his watching, spying atti-tude. Only the odour betrayed the live dog.

Kasper lived with the farmhands. He slept and ate with them and followed at their heels when they ploughed. Up and down the field he went behind the sowing-machine and harrow, and was present at milking-time, when fodder was cut and when the cattle were herded in. He liked the rhythm of work. It kept him awake and gave him good exercise. But when a flock of running partridges or a leaping hare came his way, some-thing extraordinarily menacing and alert possessed him, which he didn't know by day. What happened to him at such moments he couldn't tell, but it was irresistible, strong and delightful.

Josse himself had now and again been the cause of Kasper's inspiration. But Josse played tag with the big, clumsy dog. He understood enough to know that Kasper did not let himself be fooled by a few loopings and other tricks as easily as dogs like Tramp or Fille. He was swifter at turning and surer at following.

Fields and meadows, dikes and ditches were now at the height of their luxuriance. Josse couldn't wish for a better life.

He met with a host of other hares in the corn, many smaller than he thought a hare could be. He was still a solitary dweller, but absolute solitude was no hardship to him. He liked to be able to hear the sounds made by other creatures about him, and was glad and happy when he ran across one of his own kind. He hadn't to run far now for that!

He met Hopsy too and often sat and talked to her; but Hopsy understood so little of all Josse had to say that the conversation never lasted long. Hopsy, like himself, had gained several pounds, and Josse thought she had grown pretty. She had long projecting front teeth and a deep cleft in her underlip. But she was herself still, just what she had always been.

One day Josse met the biggest hare he had ever seen. This hare was a giant. He met him in a path in the corn, where he sat munching with quivering nostrils and cheerfully erect ears. He was coarse about the head, with big jawbones and great bulging eyes, a broad back and enormous hind quarters.

It was Lepidus, his father!

The old fellow saw the little hare coming and in a

moment began the sign speech with his ears. Lepidus talked quickly; his ear-flaps moved every moment and were thrown with lightning swiftness backwards and forwards. Josse answered brightly and talked for a long time to his parent—till Lepidus, when the conversation was in full swing, suddenly broke off and with a wild leap, loud snortings and blowings, made straight for Josse. The fact was that he suddenly realized that Josse was a buck hare—and he never could endure buck hares.

Josse didn't take this ill-treatment much to heart. He was used to worse, although he might have expected better treatment from his father.

The joy of the day entered into the foals and lambs. After a warm morning drink, when they had slaked their thirst from their mothers, they began to gambol and gallop, throwing up a shower of dew about them. On the dike near the pond Girik crowed; but he cut short his greeting to the morning, for he had a foreboding of what was about to happen.

After three weeks of steady persistent sitting, there began a murmuring in the precious eggs; the long, lonely wait was at an end and the chicks were about to hatch out.

When Girik approached his eagerly clucking little mate, he was no longer in doubt and lay down by the nest. He took the newly hatched chicks to dry them. There was a regular crowd of them; if he didn't see to it at once, they would smother one another—and his little hen hadn't yet hatched out the last egg.

Considering everything, all had gone well—and it was a proud moment when a little later in the day, followed by his mate and eighteen yellow-legged children, he led the way from the narrow nest's hollow out into the fresh air.

They were red-brown with yellow streaks and many-coloured, like the sunlit June flowers about them, and when they clucked "Teep-teep-teep" and suddenly lay down on the spot where they stood, they were like a bunch of flowers growing in the grass. One of them had some difficulty in keeping up. It was a tiny thing that seemed to be quite different from the rest. It often lay down and panted and looked as if it were suffering from indigestion. Was it a partridge chick, that little thing? Was it really the genuine progeny of proud Girik? It looked like a snail that used its feelers as legs and dragged its towering house after it.

The little chick still carried an eggshell on its back. The shell in which it had developed from a germ into a little living creature of the earth had unfortunately remained stuck to it. With every breath the chick took he grew, his muscles gained in elasticity, the wings on his back wanted to caress the air. The shell bound and oppressed the unfortunate little bird.

The hen partridge was so busy amid her other chicks, making a way through the grass for them, keeping count of them and calling them together at every moment, that she hadn't noticed the youngest of the family. With her wings half-raised, so as to cover and protect the chicks as much as possible from the glance of some long-sighted crow or from the few belated, cold dewdrops that now and then dripped down from the grass, she went forward with them.

Girik himself was farther on at the head of his army; he investigated the surroundings, warned and encouraged and showed the nearest way to the dwelling of the yellow ants.

Everything went on famously. . . .

Sometimes his hen and chicks were like a strange, long-drawn-out, fantastic beast, winding its way in haste along the dike: at others the numerous small family disbanded. Girik slowed down and the chicks scattered until Mrs. Girik, with a few warning clucks, called the whole brood together. They gathered round her, resting comfortably in shelter and warmth under the down of her belly and breast-feathers. Those that couldn't for the moment find room had to stand in a row under her protecting wing.

Meanwhile they weren't inactive in there in the darkness. Light shed a promise of loveliness amid the green grass stems about them. They knew the beating of their mother's heart, and there were other outside sounds that attracted them. A little beak came out, a head and a neck, and then three small, yellow toes. It was as though the little hen had suddenly turned into a brood of chicks. They peeped out from the shelter of her wings, and from under the roof formed by her breast; they scrambled out by the chinks between her flight feathers; they bristled from her neck; they perched on her back. She became a hedgehog of a hen, her prickles were bristling heads and beaks. All the delays were very fortunate for the little chick with the eggshell on his back, almost enabling him to keep up with the troop. While the others patiently awaited the result of their father's careful reconnaissances, he had time to get over the many difficulties that hindered him. Stones that lay in the way, that the others hopped over with agility, he had to go laboriously round. Stiff last-year's stalks that the others could slip between brought him invariably into trouble. Once he very nearly got caught by his shell, but he edged backwards, slipped free, and then looked round for the others. In careless ignorance of the dangers that lurked for such a poor little creature as he, he toiled on, and came up panting, chirping and worn out, just in time for the storming of the yellow aints' fortress.

On the top of the dike, raising its dome high over the grass, lay the ant-hill, covered with a kind of crust. Girik sprang briskly up on to it and immediately earth scattered about the chicks' ears. He rooted mightily and in a moment had scraped a breach in the dwelling. Then he clucked for his children to assemble and dealt greasy white ants' eggs out by the ounce.

The chicks had never seen an ant's egg, but they didn't hesitate about it long. They were soon as eager as Girik, and the strongest began to scrape for eggs themselves. Girik looked upon these with peculiar pride. Those must, of course, be cocks!

The little thing with the eggshell ate such immense quantities that its armoured jacket squeezed it harder than ever. The mother often aimed a blow of her beak at the shell, but the chick quite misunderstood her good intentions. New-born as it was and cruelly afflicted at that, it thought that its parent only wanted to deprive it of its chance of getting ants' eggs.

They investigated the yellow ants' hill thoroughly. Girik found such abundant stores of eggs that it never entered his head to move from the hill. So long as *he* could scrape and find fresh titbits there were beaks to swallow them.

He stayed there with his big family the whole forenoon and when finally they were all tired they sat down for a noonday rest round the hill in the grass.

To a water-hole in the low-lying meadows where the last remains of reeds and rushes had taken refuge from

Farmer Jens Tyrbag, where the shrew-mice scurried under twigs in the winter and the heart-grass quivered and shook, Girik came on warm summer evenings at the head of his chicks and his bride.

The little pond, the bitterness of whose water all old Jens Tyrbag's industry and engenuity had not been able to get the better of, was Girik's place of refreshment and the sole place where, in peace from men, he could give vent to his exuberant, primeval nature.

Here the brick-red drain-pipe emptied itself. Here murmured and rippled refreshing streams; here the little ones could go to the water and drink.

Under the broad-headed but thin-necked, ever trembling sedge, over which flies flew lazily, the pond gleamed dull and green. The rushes rustled and rattled and long-legged frogs hopped about in the paths that wound between the kingcup stems. Somehow the little pond made one think of all the hostile things that lie in wait for young creatures of the field in every field and in every meadow. The trampled path with its prints of many paws was one of Jit-Jit the murderous weasel's sources of income.

The dike and the pond were at the very boundary of Girik's expansive realm. To the river far to the west, he only came now and then, generally in late autumn. Then the air would be full of shot, and in spite of his earnest calls and protests, large, promising and obedient chicks would make up their minds to fly upwards in flocks and would as suddenly fall with a thud to the ground.

The summer day was bright and hot.

Many different sounds came to Josse's ears as he took his day's sleep in a tuft of corn a good way from the anthill. He heard the roller's monotonous clanking from the nearest fields, the lapwings' wearisome squalling and crying, the larks' twittering, and a mole digging through the earth close to his bed. He heard each crow of a cock or bay of a dog from the village on the hill. Every sound that came to him: a horse, or a cow, his hearing carefully noted and investigated; and yet he was asleep.

A big, pale-yellow dog was trotting behind the roller, up and down the field, with lowered head and switching tail. It moved its legs mechanically, for it was asleep.

Racial qualities inherited from Kasper's father, the noble sporting dog with the wild temperament, always caused him to prefer to keep his legs moving.

The roller had at last finished rolling half the field and it was near dinner time in the village on the hill. The farmhand took up a clod. "Kasper, Kasper," said he, spitting upon the clod with a fierce look in his eyes and throwing it far into a patch of corn. Dutifully Kasper made his three or four "fetch" jumps and went off into the corn, the tall ears of which tickled his flanks quite pleasantly.

When he had made his way through the corn to the place where he thought the clod lay, he suddenly saw it quiver and come alive.

A fiery gleam came into his eye, a hunting bay rose in his throat, and his paws ached to leap, as at night when he was guarding the garden and the farmyard and measuring out strict justice among the village cats. He was at once fire and flame. And now he was on the clod's track!

But it was only Josse, who the whole morning had followed Kasper's slow movements. While he was getting up speed he made a series of challenging bobs with his head and flicked his white tail coquettishly in the air.

He hopped lightly on his toes; he leaped so agilely and

elastically that his paws only just had time to print their mark on the earth. A superfluity of strength was in him, and his legs moved without his being conscious of their movement.

Kasper came on behind, slowly, but surely. He hadn't a first-class nose and he often lost the scent; but his persistence passed all bounds, his father's spirit and passion drove him forward over stock and stone, every fibre taking part in the pursuit. He worked his way forward, announcing loudly the way little Josse had taken.

"Here the rascal ran round the mound," he bayed.

"Yes, that's right," thought Josse, listening to him from afar.

"Here he had a nice rest for a moment; he was in among the willows, and he sat down and thought."

"Yes, that's quite right too," thought Josse.

So it went on for a long time; until all at once Kasper bayed at the top of his voice.

"Here the rascal hopped backwards and forwards over the brook. He wanted to trick me."

Oh, that gave Josse a terrible shock! For he found that the dog could follow all his loopings. But now the baying hound was quite close to the place where he lay and he dared not stay there any longer. He sprang up and scurried off.

Very nimbly and very lightly went the clever paws over the earth, and his heart beat terribly hard in his body. But he was now more careful and sparing of his strength, keeping cunningly to the thick grass, where he made every kind of loop and bend in order to escape his pursuer.

With quivering ears and swinging tail Kasper thudded his feet on the earth behind him. The wind was favourable to his mediocre scent and enabled him to hold on.

He looked like a yellow stream meandering through the corn. His pulses beat hard and the spittle scattered in little showers from his red, streaming tongue. From time to time he bayed and then galloped off again faster than ever after Josse.

But Josse had legs too—and he had eyes and ears as well, which showed that he had begun to be a thinking being. So many had been his nightly excursions that he knew quite well that the more swiftly he ran and the more lightly he trod, the more quickly did his tracks become scentless and cold. He remembered too from his adventure with Fille that big ditches and water broke the scent, and when, in the course of his flight, he had got half round the hill on which the village stood, an idea came into his head and he increased his speed.

He knew quite well where he was. The lime pits lay on one side; the blackthorn bushes and the old ruined house on the other. If he kept on by ditch and hollow, straight in front of him, he would come to the hawthorn, to the pond, to the lapwings. He had his plan clear. Just then he heard a new dog's bark in front of him. It was the booming, hollow bass which, almost from his birth, had given a daily concert to the fields where his infancy had been spent. It was Tramp who was barking. But where was he?

Josse stopped—raised himself on the tips of his toes and listened with eagerly working nostrils and strained ears; he sniffed and spied both behind and before him.

Behind, to his great joy, Kasper was becoming less insistent. Josse turned both ears in that direction—yes! He was sure he was right. The dog was whining rather than barking now and there was no more fury in his bay. He had lost the track and was about to give up.

But Tramp, who was in front of him, was still on the

landscape. Where was *he?* Over there behind the rye, or behind the oats?

Josse listened for a long time, but the ferocious bass on the hill had stopped.

Josse didn't think it advisable to go on to the hollow, so he turned round, jogging along by the boundary fence. He came to a field of grass that was full of un-gnawed tufts and was just about to consult his somewhat weary feet as to whither he should betake himself now, when Tramp with a bellow jumped up out of a ditch.

A rat! A rat! The joy of it shone in his crafty little pig's eyes, and teeth and tongue watered with the ex-pectation of a speedy meal.

Josse was in the open field. On all sides the clover was partly cropped, partly mown. The old house with its garden full of brushwood was his nearest shelter. The great, long-legged beast was gaining fast upon him. He had no choice; he must make the best of his way to the place where, unseen by his enemy, he could make mis-leading cross-tracks and try to bring off one or two of his infallible tricks.

But Tramp, who guessed his intention and knew that the game was up if once he lost sight of the "rat," rushed like a flood crossways in between the blackthorn bushes after him. Josse turned and twisted, trying as best he could to carry out his earlier intention. He might play this vulgar bellower a trick!

At the right moment he leaped free of the blackthorn bushes and raced along a twisting path through a laby-rinth of elders, where he played a dangerous game of puss-in-the-corner with his ferocious pursuer. All at once, agilely and noiselessly, he hopped up on top of a heap of big, sharp-cornered stones, and tried out a few steps of dancing.

A reek of weasels rose to his nostrils, and for a brief second he felt a terrifying omen. As quickly as possible he jumped down off the dancing-stone, just as Tramp approached the stone heap from the other side.

Tramp blundered up over the heap of stones. Was he suffering from delusions? He had just seen a rat there, so there must be one; he went round and stuck his nose down every possible chink and crack; he sniffed and snorted, so that there was a regular draught through the cairn. Straw and leaves flew all about.

Meanwhile Josse disappeared unseen among the elders.

The weasels who lived among the stones had remained quietly in their lair. Only a few short, sharp squeals when the dog's nose came too near one of them showed that Josse's dancing had disturbed them in their daytime sleep; but now Tramp made them wide awake. He greeted his discovery of a whole family of rats with muffled growling and barking.

Then the weasels began to make a move.

They scurried agilely along the long, covered way into the safe depths of their fortress. Tramp heard their rustling in a moment and old Jit-Jit's cat-like hiss. He became more and more determined to get his teeth into these rats, and he moved his short, broad, blunt nose from chink to chink. Once he was certain that if only he could have wedged his snout a little deeper in, he could have laid hold of the rats with his front teeth.

Then he felt a slash in one of his ear-lobes and with a furious roar he drew back his head. He did it so quickly that Jit-Jit, who had come to the help of her distressed little ones, was hauled halfway out. Tramp shook his head with a great flapping of ears, but the mother weasel had let go long since.

Tramp didn't give up. His crafty eyes shone green

and red and foam edged his yellow-toothed jaws. He would teach those rats! He thrust his broad paws vigorously in among the stones and managed to break part of the heap away.

But there were still hiding-places for the long, lithe animals.

Suddenly one of the little weasels, rolled into a ball, and fell out of the stone heap. Tramp caught hold of its little stump of a tail. It cried and howled and twisted about his nose like an eel. But after her little one came Jit-Jit. In a fury she fastened herself on to his muzzle, so that he had to let go to free his head. But his chance had gone!

What weasels lack in strength they make up for in agility. At one time they all sallied out and darted round his legs like living fire. He wanted to snap them up, shake them and throw them high in the air; but they were too quick for him to get a chance to catch hold of their carrotty bodies.

He had to give it up and content himself with the knowledge that he had increased his already great experience of rats. Not everyone had such luck! With the hairs on his back bristling and stiff legs, grumbling and gradually retreating, he slowly left the neighbourhood of the stone heap.

A little hare had played him a trick—he had to accept the fact. But at least he had escaped the vixen's fate of being literally led by the nose.

Josse had come off best again. While his mean pursuer was fighting with the weasels he raced back the way he had come. When he perceived that his trick had been successful, he indulged his liking for philosophy on a hillock. Now he would carry out his plan and follow the ditch to find a place where he could stay in peace for the rest of the day. Could he find such a place? Yes, he had it. The pond—the pond!

Girik on the dike near the pond was calling his chicks together; he must take them out, down to the water. After the noon rest the little ones began to get thirsty. Then suddenly he sood up stiffly, with his head to the wind, and stretched out his neck; there was a rumbling in the earth that seemed to say that something was coming in haste along the dike. It was Josse on his way to the pond.

The old hen uttered a warning cluck, and Girik made it clear in a moment that he would fly at the head of the owner of those silly legs. All the chicks crept into hollows in the grass.

But Josse, who wanted to get away and sleep, didn't allow himself to be stopped—with a leap to one side he avoided Girik, and with his giant spring he went right over the hen and the flock of chicks. As he did so he heard something like a snail-shell crunch under one of his paws. He hurried on and made his way down among the oats, to the pond.

Afterwards, when Girik and his mate clucked the chicks together and counted them, they noticed, as the little things nestled under their breasts, that there was one which kept jumping more eagerly than the others and was never tired of flapping its wings.

It was the mite with the shell on its back. Josse had broken it. Now at last it had escaped from the egg!

CHAPTER VII

THE CAT

THE haze lifted in the east and wild roses seemed to bloom in the sky.

Day broke and its light coloured everything. The sky arched in the background over the white church tower on the hill. White-washed houses gleamed, tiles glowed, panes of glass glittered with golden light. The first rays shone on the grass, the first gleam of sunlight laid autumn's golden sheen upon the ripening rye.

Josse was running with his body lifted high and his legs held straight so as to be as far as possible from the wet earth. If he just touched an ear of corn a shower fell on him and he left, like a snail, a shiny, plainly visible path behind him. At every second hop he had to kick back with his paws to shake the water from his long, stiff ears.

Before taking his morning meal he carefully licked flower and leaf dry. He wanted to have water and food separately, and didn't appreciate dew, which only diluted the sap of the leaves.

Swallows twittered and a stork came floating by on broad, black-edged wings, followed by its mate. Flocks of sparrows eddied out from a garden hedge like dust from a sack and fell down into the middle of the corn. Young sparrows knocked against Josse's ears, they squeaked with joy and twittered and cried all together while they danced and fluttered round the ears of corn.

They had to plunge into the great, yellowish-green sea; they had to perch on something that gave way under them; and they gave the impression of little children going into the water for the first time. But with flapping wings they held their bodies up and reached out with their feet, each one for a long, thick ear which, as he caught it, swayed slowly down towards the earth with a joyous, squeaking little sparrow on its end.

More sparrows came and the first ones got tired of their chosen ears and made for others. Little sparrows bobbed up out of that sea of corn and dived down into it again.

Josse was well aware of all this twittering, but he was on his way out, far from wheat and barley, out into the uttermost fields to find himself a bed.

The heat of the summer day increased and the fragrance came from the cornfields. A white cat with coalblack tail stole from the nearest farmstead. He sauntered indolently along the broad field path.

Now and then he sat down, curled his tail gracefully round his flanks, and gazed at the countryside about him as if surveying a kingdom. Cows stood in a row and munched dutifully. The dew had now quite disappeared from the grass, so the cat had come too late for the morning milking!

Well, let that go! He was in the humour for hunting —even a mouse wouldn't come amiss.

Some holes in the grazed part of the field tempted him to hunt mice, and he stole into a hiding-place in the nearest tuft of clover. There he lay comfortably and watched. His face took on a thoughtful expression; his ears were erect . . . for the time being he was just enjoying the summer.

A little later his neck stiffened curiously, while his ears pointed in one direction. For a long time he waited expectantly.

There was a tiny rustle down under the earth. So delicate were the cat's senses that he knew when the mouse thought of coming up.

He didn't lie close to the hole—no, he lay three or four times his own length away from it. And now he perceived that the mouse was just at the surface—and he slowly raised the forepart of his body.

The mouse was out—he heard its legs rustling in the grass—and he raised himself on his four legs and stretched out his neck and body, while the tip of his tail quivered feverishly.

Three paces away he stood still. He was trembling with eagerness . . . the mouse was coming of its own accord within reach of his claws. He had only to wait and listen!

The cat made himself so long—so long; he stretched out his head in the direction of the mouse. He raised his shoulder blades and then, all at once, he sprang and fixed the claws of his forefeet in a clod of earth at the foot of a cluster of daisies. The mouse was *behind* the clump.

He had miscalculated his spring! He looked round shyly and ashamed.

Was there a witness? Was there anyone who could poke fun at him, who could proclaim his failure? And so he made off as quickly as he could, wishing the earth would open up and swallow him.

Like a wisp of mist he disappeared into a patch of rye close by, found a furrow and stole on along it. His limbs glided on elastically, noiselessly. His neck was stretched out and his ears held watchfully forward. He was closely investigating his surroundings and at the same time becoming intoxicated with the perfume of the yellow mustard. Suddenly he started. A little ladybird had lost its way in his sensitive whiskers; he had to stand still and brush them. Near him was a place where the corn was sparse. He felt uncomfortably uncovered and was across it in a jiffy. He never moved straight forward, but always went round in curves with his bent head covered by the grass at the base of the corn.

A little way on, in the patch of grain, Josse had found a resting place and was lying there at ease. Only a mole awakened him now and then, as it hastily excavated its galleries just below the earth's crust. In many places the galleries had fallen in and Josse could see the little black fellow's lair.

Bumble-bees, giddy with honey, hummed drowsily around him, and high above his head lark after lark hovered uttering its summer joy aloud in jubilant, far-sounding song.

The sun scorched Josse as he lay in the rye. He was haunted by bad dreams and once he had an evil vision. Out of a furrow a round head with stiff ears and yellow eyes slowly emerged. Light fell on the little ears so that they looked quite red, and across each of the sulphur-yellow eyes there was a black stroke.

Just then all Girik's eighteen chicks, which were not yet air-worthy, broke in on him. He was vexed at the disturbance. It was a time when he should be left in peace.

But he did not know his luck: the cat, which for a time had lurked and lain in wait for him, suddenly changed his mind.

Girik was at his post! As soon as the corn divided and the cat emerged, he shrieked his cry of warning—and how he threw himself courageously straight before the "monster's" nose, lay for a moment, and fluttered his wings as if he had thudded down, shot dead, from the sky!

The fierce joy of capture shone in the cat's eyes. He crouched and sprang! But Girik was no longer there. He was leading the way, limping off with weakly-moving wings over the ground.

The cat was after him with a spring, ears erect, tail swishing. He had been as sure of his bird as if he had already held it in his mouth. Again he was upon the cock, which could scarcely run. It cried and moved forward in fluttering hops. The cat imagined how, with one spring, it could catch the partridge cock in its paws!

Ha! its wing was broken!—wilder and more exultant became the cat's hunting.

Girik, whose power of pretence was matchless, was drawing the cat far from the hen and the chicks. They made off in the opposite direction, with Josse among them, as if he were one of the family. Far, far along the ditch they went, over the field path, into the oats and down to the pond, where they all hid amid the tufts of reeds or sedge.

After some time Girik came running back on half-spread wings to enjoy his triumph and his family's rescue. It was easy to guess what he had done. He had led the cat back home.

When the cat had finally discovered his blunder he was back at the farmstead.

Often now Josse met Girik and his flock. Either they ran across him or he tumbled unexpectedly down among them; and as the chicks grew up Girik took Josse's presence less and less ungraciously.

Schoolmaster Girik, who had guided him when he read his first A B C, now gave him a more advanced course of lessons. He taught his little hare acquaintance how to hide himself, how to twist and turn among the grass and reeds, how to shelter at a pinch among the gardens and thickets, and how to get to the bottom of the deep, overgrown ditches. The power of good planning and inventiveness were qualities which Josse had always possessed, and he came to be a past master in Girik's school.

When the partridges, leaving their evening meal, bustled round him and then suddenly ducked down, he ducked too, taking advantage of their watchfulness; and if he was sitting and dozing in his shelter and they rushed suddenly and breathlessly in upon him, he wasn't long in taking to his heels.

It was one of the great pieces of good fortune in his life that the partridges were his friends. Otherwise he might one fine day, for all his watchfulness, speed and cunning, have shared Lab's fate.

CHAPTER VIII

IN THE FOX'S CLUTCHES

THE ripe corn was, for Josse, a deep wood, where he hid himself whenever he was hunted headlong out of his bed.

He wasn't particularly fond of the corn. It wasn't easy to get about in. There were all kinds of obstacles in the way of his active paws.

No, the corn was more for Hopsy. She enjoyed it, she lived with it; it attracted her by its perfume and by its eternal lullaby—in fact, it absorbed her completely.

When Hopsy wanted to lie and rest quite undisturbed, she went into the wheat. The thick, dark wheat, with its expanse of closely-growing ears, afforded her substantial cover, which was just what her nature required. Wheat didn't whisper like barley, or rustle like rye, or ripple with the voice of the oats. There was a

107

peculiar, summery peace, a salutary assurance of safety, in the converse of heavy spikes and jointed stems with the wind. And peace and safety were very good when the stomach was full and the feet weary.

Every moment wings whirred over her head. Swift little fliers sketched their black contours against the sharp, white sunlight. Sometimes it was a lark, sometimes a thrush or linnet, or it was the yellow wagtail, which was now so worn out that it had come to be nothing but just tail and legs.

But it was chiefly the larks that whirred above Hopsy. They came from afar and were so queerly lumpy about their beaks. They flew briskly across the big wheat-fields, swinging to right and left. When they approached the place in the depths of the wheat where their nest lay, they slowed down and hovered with their fantails quivering above the ears.

How would they find their nest?

Day after day the surroundings changed; new ears grew on the stems, new flowers unfolded; it was no use to take note of a red corn-cockle or of a cluster of blue cornflowers. No, such rough landmarks were useless. Their eyes were differently developed: ditches, fences and fields guided them, and when they came into the neighbourhood of the place where they dwelt, each leaf displayed to them its typical difference. They could go straight down from the sky to the edge of the nest, and when, as often happened, they lingered hovering in the air over the place, it was more to mislead their enemies and spy out the surroundings than anything else.

Hopsy didn't worry about them. She dozed in the thick dark wheat, as she had always done.

Deep in the wood of corn, between fragrant bindweed, blue forget-me-not and red-brown corn-cockle hid the "witches' paths."

The witches' paths were the hares' arteries of communication; they had made them themselves in the course of the summer with their sharp front teeth that mowed down everything which stood in their way.

On those narrow, twisting paths Josse travelled when he made extensive tours of observation in these mysterious depths. By them he came evening after evening to the old mound that lay there the whole summer through with its graves, and by them he slipped along to the drinking pools and marl pits that, like oases, lay amid the yellow stems.

These paths were secret passages. The burning midday sun scarcely reached them with its rays and the cool morning wind was never felt on them. Even a falcon couldn't spy them out! But the fox and the weasel and all the cats knew them, so that when travelling along them one had generally to use one's nose.

Mrs. Reynard was prowling about on her usual evening hunt.

In the corn she had been lucky enough to come upon a mouse, and when she had been slinking along the field path, she had caught a beetle. Then she had rested for a moment and meanwhile had gone over her coat thoroughly for fleas. After that she had gone on farther through the corn, had come out into a ditch and had found the track of a cat, which, however, had escaped at full speed to the village of Bjaerg.

The vixen wanted to go to the pond, where as a rule she found something or other to gobble up. She leaped over ditches and slunk by witches' paths down towards the pond.

Josse was coming from the opposite direction, and as

he came to a turn of the path, he suddenly stood face to face with his hereditary foe. They were both so surprised that they squatted down with their eyes fixed on each other. The vixen was not without some hope that perhaps this hare would, like so many others, go crazy and from sheer flurry run right into her jaws.

She had already in thought devoured little Josse whole! Her eyes had taken note of his fleshy thighs and long, muscular body. With her ears she noted every beat of her victim's heart. With her nose she drew in his strong, sweetish, appetizing odour, and with her teeth that watered she was already eating him—so carried away was she by her sense-perceptions!

The vixen hated this Lepidus family—all of them, both big and small—she hated them when she was far away from them and when they outran her and tricked her before her very nose; but she loved them so much that she simply rocked with pleasure and joy when she had one of them under her paws and made its delicate sides writhe between her teeth.

The tension between Josse and the vixen soon reached its peak. The whole affair lasted at most a couple of seconds. In a flash Josse turned and made off so quickly that the vixen scarcely realized that the little hare was gone. Josse was so used to taking to his heels! Every chance meeting here amid the grain all through the summer might well be, and frequently was, a matter of life and death, and he naturally used *his* weapons. Once he was in flight he could easily get clear away; he would find some hiding-place and make good his escape.

But he didn't need his tricks this time; the vixen knew what she was about: better a beetle in hand than one of that Lepidus family in the bush. She would get another chance.

The grain was nearly ripe. The rye was ripe already; its long stems could no longer carry the heavy ears; they bent and leaned on each other with the tips of the ears all close to the earth. The spikes, which had been so soft before, were now rough and hard, and the brown kernels of the rye projected from their husks. Now and then at midday, when gusts of wind went through the corn, ripe grains hailed down on Hopsy.

But Josse followed his path in spite of the fox and old Lepidus. Every evening and morning he ran under the triumphal arches of the rye.

The grain was tumbling down over his head; autumn was beginning; and it was as if all the bustle of Bjaerg was extended to the fields. There was hissing, cracking and rumbling about him. There was the noise of the air-generator at the mill, of the smith's anvil, the calling and shouting of the farmhands, all of which had been until now a distant, subdued chorus. Now all this was suddenly about him. Big, automatic binders rumbled and beat their wings—"sikke-sakke, sikke-sakke" they went every moment.

At night he ventured up to one of them and sniffed at it. It ate corn, he could see. Many of them had stuffed themselves to such an extent that big tufts stuck out of their throats. He vaulted over the tail of the thing; as he did so, he smelt horse and binding yarn, harness and grease, and sweat from the grasp of the farmhands. He raised himself up as high as he could and took a general look over the sleeping *sikke-sakke*. He found out that it was a strange kind of creature that slept if the farmhands didn't pull its legs and tail.

One day the rye fell; shortly afterwards the barley; then the wheat and oats. Incomprehensible happenings!

The earth became bare and empty.

Wherever one went in the fields, there was Farmer Tyrbag or his farmhands.

Hopsy found refuge in the close ranks of the turnips. Lepidus, who knew what was happening, retreated to the marshes, where he was wont at such times to adopt the water rat's, the otter's, and the stray domestic cat's way of living. But Josse, who when it all began had been just as confused as Hopsy, took up the matter with his boasted superiority and carefree serenity. By degrees he realized that the landscape in its new aspects had new joys to offer.

Now he had the freedom of his paws; he could leap about everywhere. When evening came and the fields were quiet he set forth with frisky hops over the new stubble. Many comrades were there too, and they had a good time playing tag merrily among the shocks of corn. He was easily the best vaulter. He had one leap in which he threw his back legs up high behind him. It looked as if he were, in a way, stretching his legs after sleep. Then there was another leap which he tried when the weather was good and when he was particularly jubilant and full of spirits: he sprang straight up into the air, throwing his forelegs far out before him. He also practised making sudden turns. He zigzagged forward at such speed that he formed a cross of grey streaks above the earth. But as it became darker and darker his body could be seen less and less—and finally one could only see the gleam of his white, flapping ears.

The full moon was near its setting. Jens Tyrbag's wheat that stood in tall shocks was becoming yellower and drier under its husks. It was already day and a rosy gleam of light was creeping over the horizon. Sound and colour heralded its coming. Cocks crowed and geese cackled in Bjaerg. Over yonder—but there came a gust

The Fox

of wind rustling the turnip leaves above Josse's head. It stifled every other sound. It was a fresh, windy, dewy dawn.

Josse sat in one of the closest rows. He had always liked turnips so much! He gnawed off mouthful after mouthful and enjoyed that strong, fresh morning feeling. His legs were a bit tired, for he and the vixen had been at odds during the night. This usual nightly game of puss-in-the-corner had this time taken a serious form. The fox had been tricked, of course! Nobody could get the better of Josse.

But the vixen tried her luck again.

The turnip leaves on Josse's lee side began to rustle and two little erect, broad-topped ears shot up among them. A moment later a black nose-tip slowly rose into the air and a pair of glittering eyes peeped out. The whole familiar fox-face suddenly appeared out of the green depths of the turnip field. The moist, dribbling lower jaw, which hung a little down, gave the face a sardonic grin. The cunning vixen couldn't restrain her joy at seeing her little friend Josse so near!

She already felt that the little hare's life was in her power; the wind was favourable to her; it blew from her prey and she could traverse the slight distance that still separated them with a couple of springs. Each time the unsuspecting Josse made a couple of hops to another turnip and stuck his head down into cover to take a gnaw, the fox crept swiftly towards him with her belly gliding along the earth. But when Josse raised himself, she lay stiff and motionless.

The morning wind rustled the leaves and whirled them about, making a noise like the sea, a rushing, a singing, a plashing.

Then the vixen sprang! At last she had won the game!

She held Josse fast with her forefeet, but the turnips prevented her from biting. Josse's loose, hairy, smooth coat also made it difficult for the old vixen, whose claws and teeth were no longer so very sharp, to hold him fast.

Meanwhile Josse was making sounds that were a delight to her ears. He shrieked and wailed so that Hopsy, who was sitting and eating in the vicinity, came up. Like Josse, when the weasel caught Lab, curiosity drew her to the spot. She had to come and find out more about these sounds. The sight of the vixen at once put her on her guard. The sight of Josse writhing in her clutches held her rooted to the spot.

And now she began to run round and round the shrieking Josse. She had not the strength to help him; but her primitive instinct urged her to lend her unfortunate brother a helping hand.

Her intention to fool the vixen until she let go was not conscious. It was, rather, something she *had* to do, something that lay, like an inherited tendency, deep in her nature. But the result was that the vixen, to whose greed there was no limit, let go her hold of Josse, whom she supposed to be sufficiently incapacitated, and made a sudden sally against Hopsy.

Hopsy hopped off without preparation, without a preliminary run—straight from the spot where she sat. The elastic spring in her back legs carried her, bunched together like a clod of earth, far away into the field. Snarling with greed, the vixen made after her, while Josse, still unharmed and lively, lost no time in seeking safety in flight.

But the vixen lost Hopsy, and Josse had disappeared.

For a long time the old vixen sniffed round the place where Josse had been and vainly hunted through the turnip plantation.

Like the cat she was ashamed; but she gave herself up to the enjoyment of the bits of Josse's coat which she had torn off. This was not only a precautionary measure, to allay suspicion, but also a satisfaction. Anyhow, they tasted of hare skin!

Josse was somewhat tender after the many blows and nips he had received. His haughty spirit deserted him for many days. He hid himself well away either at the bottom of a dry ditch or among the tufts of rushes or sedge by the pond. Here he sat and grew wise. His adventure in the fox's clutches affected him far more deeply than the weasel's teeth in his neck; but it also gave him a much higher degree of knowledge.

He limped about painfully for a week; but from that day forward he never failed, when he got the fox's acrid scent, to be so alarmed that he shook all over his body.

CHAPTER IX

THE SCOURGE TO HARES

THE Danish fields were enjoying their autumn rest. Yellow sunshine, the summer heat of which had vanished with the first showers of the cool September days, alternated with big, white, puffy clouds so that light and shadows alternately swept over the earth. A fresh wind whistled through the seeding weeds under the hedges and hummed in the poplars and willows on the farms. Now and then lapwings assembled in flocks and all the larks had gone silent; there was the deep hum of the autumn wind in the hedges.

Secure in its harvest and in its flaming yellow fields lay the little village of Bjaerg. Field-mice ate until they grew quite round; Girik's chicks were already big and strong; and Josse, Lepidus, and Hopsy were rivals at eating.

As he walked, Jens Tyrbag felt the heavy ears of corn, and Fille, who was with him, looked after the mice. Degnen the hunter made flocks of partridges rise. Lord, how big and plentiful they were! Everything rejoiced. All was well.

In Bjaerg there was a dog whose name was Lyn and whose acquaintance Josse hadn't yet made. Fortunately he had avoided coming across it, although it was to be found daily in most parts of the parish. It was a slender, long-legged pointer with a fine, glossy, chalk-white skin, on which were sprinkled big orange-coloured spots.

The farmhand with whom it lived said it had a very fine pedigree. He had got it from a smallholder out by the big marsh, one of the best-known hunters in the district, whose dogs were so good that they were hired out when fine folk came to shoot over the marsh.

Anyhow, the dog was the scourge to hares, and, led by its good, sharp nose and driven by its sleepless desire for the chase, it spent hours longing for the time when it might set off with its nose to the earth. What it caught it liked to kill, and what it didn't catch it tried to hunt far beyond its lawful hunting-grounds.

The pointer was fussing round the field that afternoon. From moment to moment it stood still with one paw lifted and then went on. Sniffing loudly and with its tail whisking from side to side, it raced down from the hillock where Josse had lain in the morning to the ditch where he had eaten his last leaf. Josse noticed that it was eager and quick. Now it was over by the hedge; now down by the water; it was making for him. In the present case he didn't know quite what to do. This dog was a stranger. Had it been Fille, Tramp or Kasper, he would in any case have remained sitting quietly for a while, thinking over all his cunning tricks and leaps. But with this fellow he was in doubt, and when he was in doubt there was nothing for it but to show a clean pair of heels. Off he went in a moment with high, frisky, mad hops. He ran quickly down the hill. He didn't go the direct, steep way, but by a slanting path, so as not to run the risk of tumbling head over heels.

A fresh, cool wind blew about him and put him in the mood for a good run. His paws were delighted to have leave to go. At this time of day they were thoroughly rested and had grown weary of being still.

Hop, hop, hop . . . the whole mechanism of his little body hummed; his paws gripped the earth more swiftly than his eyes could see the ground over which he ran. Only his good nose gave him a hint now and then as to what he was passing over.

He had already passed the stubble, and noticed the faint distant smell of the marsh's strong, delicious, spicy plants—sweet mint and baldrian. His skin slipped as if oiled over his moving bones. His lungs drew in the air in full breaths; his paws, as they worked, made a clear, humming sound, beating out the melody that had been the theme of Josse's life up to now, and his long, erect ears listened contentedly while they played backwards and forwards in time to the tune: hop, hop, hop!

The dog from Bjaerg village was after him. It didn't run like other dogs, but in mighty, space-devouring, curved leaps. If it was chasing a hare across an open field it seldom failed to catch it. It didn't hurry. The scourge of hares had time; the race itself was a joy and the hunt a pleasure, a pastime and at the same time an exercise for the muscles. Its heart was full of ecstasy because it had some work to do at last. The low-lying land down by the big marsh spread, a long, even expanse, before Josse.

His paws knew this. He had shown them the flat lands so often! After a series of swift leaps his sense of smell suddenly reminded him that if he swung to the right he would come upon a close plantation of turnips with big, broad leaves. To the right, then, to the right! That way there was cover!

He made an agile turn and kicked friskily out behind him. Then his vigilant ears informed him that there were men among the turnips.

In a flash he changed his direction.

"The path," cried his paws, which had now suddenly remembered the field path across the valley.

The pointer's pleasure is in hunting. For it, sport is chasing every running wild creatures that it lays its eyes on, until that creature lies still and trembling.

The marsh and shelter among the reeds were unfortunately not for Josse just then. He had to take a roundabout way: there were too many men in his path. Out across the valley work was going on at such a pace that the wind of it beat on his ears.

A little way on, just in the direction in which he was going, there were three small holdings in a row. Should he go through them or by them? He must decide at once. He must have reasonable room for his turn and, in case he chose to go through, he must beware lest he should come too close to the house where Rask, the snappy foxterrier, lived. He made his decision and turned in the direction he had chosen.

But Lyn, who hunted with his eyes almost as much as with his nose, saw at once that the little brown creature he was hunting had decided to swerve inwards and he also saw that, if the whole matter wasn't settled at once, his prospective victim would escape him. So he suddenly put on a tremendous spurt in order to intercept Josse when he passed in front of the house.

Josse made his way into the garden's thick jungle of dog-roses, blackberry, and thorn bushes. From his many adventures with Bjaerg dogs, he knew by experience that dogs didn't like the pricking of thorns on their noses and skins.

But hunted as he was, he could see no further means of safety. He went on across the garden and over the heaps of earth and manure that lay close to the little greenhouse, and then across the panes of the greenhouse roof. Lyn followed, and Rask, furious over this intrusion into his domain, followed too. The glass was not strong enough to bear Lyn and he fell through. But Rask got right up on to the roof and Josse had to make a flying leap down into a neighbouring thicket. He had been hunted to a standstill and knew quite well what he was doing. It was dangerous to hop. Very well, branches and leaves would take him under their protection; they would tear his lips and forehead, but for the rest would keep him safe and sound. But Rask remained standing irresolutely on the edge of the roof, looking down. At last he began to bark, just for something to do.

Then the man of the house came up. All he saw was Rask on the roof of the greenhouse, but neither Josse nor Lyn. He thought the devil had got into the dog. For the broken plants and all the other damage unlucky Rask had to bear the blame. "Rask, Rask!" cried the man furiously . . . and the poor fellow nearly had the life shaken out of him.

But Josse went on through the hedges and Lyn after him with bleeding shanks. Unfortunately the pointer had done himself no further damage. He hunted more fiercely and swiftly than before.

"The marsh, the marsh," ran through Josse's head all the while. The marsh had been his first idea, his original plan; and what he had once got into his head always stayed there hard and fast. He would go to the marsh: it was just straight on to it: he was on the way.

This time luck was on his side. The way stood open, a long spring shot him swift as an arrow down to the brook, but he had no time to try the temperature of the water with his paws. He had to go right in. When he had swum across, he darted into the shelter of the willows and bog myrtle and reeds and rushes and heard Lyn racing after him.

Suddenly there was a perceptible vibration somewhere above him. He smelt something worse than the pointer! There was no doubt of it—it was another enemy! The vixen!

The fox was sleeping her day sleep in the part of the marsh which Josse had entered, where no turf-cutter would disturb her rest. For a moment she didn't know what it was all about. She scented a hare and saw it; suddenly there was a dog too. She must look alive and must wake up and look out for herself. For from being a scourge to hares, Lyn, who was very fickle-minded, had changed into a fox-hunter.

With relaxed muscles and beating heart, Josse drew in the air in short, quick gasps. He had stopped under a willow and was getting his breath back. Everything was quiet and peaceful about him. His body ceased to shake with fright and he saw life in a friendly, rosy light. No dog did *him* any harm, and no dog could catch him; no cat, no weasel, no fox—or at any rate no fox, once he had taken to his heels. He knew that, he believed it, so absolutely exultant did he feel at that moment.

Unfortunately a little later in the day he noticed the

vixen's scent. From his refuge under the grey willow between the bog myrtle and the reeds he suddenly heard a frightful noise in the thicket. There was crunching and cracking and now and then the wind wafted to him the smell of fox and dog. The pursuit was, he noted, continuing; the race he had taken part in was still in progress from one end of the marsh to the other. At length, however, the noise ceased.

But his craftiness was mightily increased after this adventure. He began to be sure of a thing he had long suspected; that not only can one hide one's scent by throwing oneself into another animal's scent, but one can also, if one is really crafty, make another take on the whole danger.

When the evening fell in the fields and the larks one by one came down into the stubble, Josse knew that the autumn day was over. In the red light of the sunset he departed.

He hopped back to the place he had come from, to the Bjaerg fields; this time he *didn't* swim the brook but crossed by a bridge. When he came near the ridge of the hill where he had sat that morning, he saw Lyn limping homewards by a field path.

For once the pointer had had no luck.

CHAPTER X

THE GREATEST ENEMY

THICK, clammy mists wreathed the grass and stubble one wet, grey September morning. . . .

Old Mother Lepidus was slipping across the mound. She stole between the open stone coffins, by the big gravestones on which all kinds of rubbish, bits of glass and old household utensils were now thrown; on along by dripping hedges of bird-cherry trees. She came to a gravel pit, where the great mullein in masses, with its last yellow lanterns, gleamed above a billowing sea of cobwebs, and hopped in among the withered potato-plants. Her sharp teeth nibbled with great relish a run-to-seed dandelion which stood in her way. Its down, too wet to blow off, clung closely to her coat.

Then she hid behind a bordering hedge between bog myrtle and blackberry bushes.

The mist above her head became thinner and thinner. The day grew bright and sunny.

As the sun rose higher, the air became warmer. It was full of the humming of bees and the sleepy lowing of cows in the distance.

The old mother hare, after a fruitful summer, was preparing to enjoy her winter rest and make herself comfortable in her chosen nest. She had Hopsy's nature; she was *trustful*.

Suddenly she awoke; but too late. A little man with a gun ready was walking round and round her retreat.

She held herself uneasily with her head drawn into her body and her long ears laid flat along her back. Her bristling muzzle was held low, and the hair was smooth on her body. Hers was not the downy growth of a young hare, to betray her when suddenly stirred by the wind. Her yellow eyes moved round in her head, as she followed every movement of the man.

A party of sportsmen from Bjaerg, under the leadership of the parish clerk, had been informed by Niels' shepherd-boy where she had settled that morning. In consequence, after a time a party had assembled, and the more bloodthirsty of its members had levelled their guns.

"No! Stop!" said the parish clerk, who was a sportsman. "No assassination!"

The tailor, as the most enthusiastic of the party, was to have the right to shoot her.

"But not in her form, of course," added the parish clerk. "Let the hare leap first."

They were all closely watching the good tailor's movements.

The tailor actually thought that he, with his meek, simple, mild eyes that really never dared to look a man in the face, could, if he concentrated, fascinate a hare. He went round and round the place where he knew she must lie, circling more and more narrowly round his victim.

Suddenly his eyes met those of Mother Lepidus. He looked into her big, round, yellow eyes and saw her slanting black pupils quivering with strained anxiety. It gave the little sportsman a terrible shock. He had never before been near enough to a hare to meet its eyes.

The serious amber eyes were staring at him; each eye expressed fear and dread. They sparkled and glittered with the concentrated desire to escape. The tailor suddenly felt tense. His nerves quivered, his knees shook. If anyone ever had palpitation of the heart, he had it then!

It was the first day of hare-hunting and, possibly for that reason, the tailor was particularly eager and impatient. The old mother hare had no idea that the peace of her fields was about to be shattered. Perhaps that was why she was so dignified and still, her eyes fixed, with a steady assurance on her adversary.

The tailor was so excited he could not bring the gun into position and moved round and round the spot where the hare lay. He dared not kick the hare to make her move.

At last the critical moment came when his nerves could endure the strain no longer. He relaxed, and the look in his mild eyes flashed with lightning swiftness a message to the experienced mother hare.

She sprang! She shot forward with the swiftness of a shooting star.

Something flickered before the sight of the enthusiastic tailor-sportsman. He saw as it were a whole row of hares racing through the grass. But now that the situation was developing rapidly he couldn't keep up with it.

So his first shot went into the earth at least a yard from the hare. This increased the eager marksman's flurry. He hurriedly shot again and missed—for the hare was nearly twenty yards away.

It was Mrs. Lepidus's great good fortune—the greatest she had had that year—that in this effective and very instructive manner she had been warned of the beginning of the shooting season.

In the course of the summer, when no man had ever done her any harm, she had become very tame and confident; of all her many enemies the man was by no means the most dangerous. Now the shooting season had come and things were changed.

And she was not the only mother hare to fear the hunting season. When the young ones had got safely through the first critical weeks, they became nearly as crafty as their elders, and they all became aware that when a man wasn't following a horse or a cow, was not with a plough or a roller, he was dangerous.

Until the shooting began, the one who knew this lesson least was Josse. Fox, dog, cat and weasel—yes, if one saw one of them, one was bound to take care; but man—a creature whose legs seemed incapable of speed—was he —*he*—really an enemy?

Behind the turnips in the oat-stubble sat Josse in a hollow where the big, rust-spotted coltsfoot leaves were thickest. The newly mowed grass made a green wood about him. He sat in his form, well hidden.

Girik and his wife and chicks came swarming in on Josse. They came as fast as their legs could carry them. They had made themselves very small, drawn in their necks, bent their knees, and they glided noiselessly to and fro.

Now there was a rustling in the stubble and he heard

the pattering and brisk jumping of paws. He let his ears drop down lower and lower along his neck and humped his loins. The tumult among the chicks ceased in a moment. He threw himself down on his stomach and stole a glance in the direction of the sound.

The noise had stopped. A sporting dog which had long been on the track of the running birds had at last found them. He stood there, a few leaps from them, with head and tail raised. There they lay, looking toward him, where the rust-red coltsfoot clustered thickest and a green forest of sprouts rose.

Girik lay foremost, but in the midst of the flock and nearest to Josse was the little hen. She dared to raise her head for a quick nervous glance; yes, there were steps and trampling and the sound of voices in the fields.

The hunters came up briskly, their guns ready. Girik knew he was surrounded and could delay no longer. He gave the signal—"Up!"—and there was a crackling and a screeching all round. Wings whirred, the air was full of rustling, and Girik, too, made off for dear life. But the sportsmen shot three of the chicks.

All this noise made Josse nervous. The scared partridges' arrival, the reports of the guns, and Girik's shrill, alarming cries made him realize that life had become more difficult since the fields were bare and open. He must be more cautious and look out better.

It was October.

Josse was sleeping soundly by the pond. Behind the hillocks, up among the turnips, Girik was using all his arts to lead his wife and chicks from refuge to refuge.

A couple of dogs had smelled them out and now Girik was scurrying away with the whole flock along the rows of turnips. He slipped from one row to an-

other under the roof of leaves and found where the
turnips grew thinnest and where it was most open. In
the open spaces the light-yellow legs of Girik and his
family ran more easily and freely.

Away along an overgrown ditch he led them, into a
field and down over fallow ground and then along the
bottom of a deep rut and across a field path. Then he
took them down into a hollow, where they rose in flight
and flew a long way through the air, alighting in the
sedge near the pond. They hid themselves so well that
no falcon could see them and lay there resting for a
long time.

But the dog found them out and stood by till the
sportsmen came up.

Girik, with the biggest and strongest chicks, stole
away to one side; his hen, with the smaller and weaker
ones, tried to escape on the other. Then a dog sprang
into the middle of the pond and drove them up to the
greedy marksmen.

But they took comfort from the wind's song among
the stiff sedge—the free wind which they could rely
upon. The wind assured them that it would bear them
easily eastward . . . up high, where it drove the clouds
across the sky. If the earth burned beneath them, they
had but to take a leap into the air and make a couple
of strokes with their wings, while their red-brown fantails quivered! Was there not safety for them up there—
from cat, from fox. "Up, then, into the wind," cried old
Girik.

Lightly, agilely, gracefully, they rose above the tuft
where they had been sitting, with a firm faith in their
capacity for flying. Like great variegated flowers they
sprang suddenly out of their refuge among the reeds.

The guns thundered. The shot whistled and robbed

now one, now another, of tufts of feathers. Those that were hit and fell underwent a sudden transformation. They became mere clods while still in the air, little clods of foolhardy earth that had ventured up into the air and now with increasing speed were rushing down to the soil again.

Greedy dogs' jaws gripped the clods—one dog who was particularly greedy ran in among the reeds and ate his share of the booty.

"Snapper, you lout!" shouted the sportsmen threateningly at the dog: a big, fierce, short-haired beast. But Snapper, who had been chained up all through the summer and hadn't caught even a leveret or a mouse, was now harvesting his share of the year's wild crop.

The sportsmen separated. Those with the dogs went forward again to get the birds that had gone in the direction of the lime pits, but one zealous hunter wanted to tramp over the grazing grounds.

On the way one of Girik's chicks, that had separated itself from the flock and had been lying in a little clump of reeds, rose. The sportsman winged him and had to go after him. As he was blundering about, looking for the bird, he approached the place where Josse was sitting and came up and kicked his tuft. Then Josse leaped.

Josse wasn't as yet a full-sized buck hare; but he was quite a nice little breakfast hare, as the sportsman saw, and he sent a shot after him. There was a faint "click, click!"—not the usual thundering report.

While the man had been blundering round after Girik's winged chick, he had forgotten to close his gun; fine sand from a dry molehill had got into its mechanism and the grains of sand had prevented the trigger from releasing the deadly cartridge.

"Confound it all!" swore the sportsman angrily, but then immediately consoled himself.

"Oh, well, it was only a *little* hare."

By night the fox hunted in the fields and the weasel and the cat lay in ambush in the overgrown ditches.

By day the sportsman tramped about and his dog searched, while falcon and hawk from their high places spied poor Josse out. He was persecuted more than anyone; they all wanted to catch him, they all wanted to eat him; it was astonishing that the little fellow was still alive.

CHAPTER XI

THE PACK

IN the early dawn Josse was out for the sole purpose
of listening.

A damp mist blew low over the earth, and the greensward on the half-grazed pasture was covered with a
grey veil.

The sky was cloudless. Josse could hardly see the
lark that rose from its tuft before him. He saw its white
belly gleam and heard a few twitters: the rest of the
bird—its brown body and brown wings—were merged
in the greyness. Partridges that lay before his nose flew
up and flapped their wings into his very ear; but they
too were merged in the all-pervading grey.

Loud, hoarse caws sounded over his head. Out of the
dark air came four crows and thudded down on to the
ground. For a moment they sat motionless with out-

stretched necks and stiff beaks; then they began to waddle about with wide, awkward strides. They were not dangerous now to Josse. He was too big.

The day broke, slowly becoming more transparent and brighter. The moon grew pale and shrank; it disappeared as if into its case.

Josse had been all round the neighbourhood and had seen with regret that the farmhands, after having taken the corn from the fields when the ears were full, were now ploughing up the roots.

He was sitting half way up a slope, where there was cover, and he saw the red sun like some gigantic fruit from which the wind has dried the dew. Slowly it emerged from the thick grey cloud. He shook himself and warmed himself in its rays. Would he have his day's rest that day, he wondered!

At the end of October, when all the hares were full-grown, the parish organized a general shoot.

Everyone in Bjaerg met together; farmers and householders, tailors, smiths and painters; everyone who could carry a gun.

But as, even so, there were not enough of them, each inhabitant of the parish had had leave to invite a guest.

The guests were as a rule sportsmen from the nearest country town. One local man came with his greengrocer, another with his middleman. If a man had a doctor who was a sportsman, he was of course invited, as were also lawyers, veterinary surgeons and cattle commissioners. Postcards were always sent out well in advance so that people could arrange their plans accordingly.

The day came and a red sun in a bright sky promised the most beautiful weather.

Long before the hour fixed men with guns began to

meet, on foot, in carts, in cars and on bicycles. Lyn's master, who walked about with his dog on a leash, constituted himself the president of the shoot and welcomed the others.

A considerable troop of sportsmen had soon assembled. There was no lack of dogs: the Bjaerg pack was quite satisfactory. There was scarcely one missing. Kasper promenaded with his pale, straw-coloured skin, together with Kora, Tramp and Fille; Kasper had an inkling of what was going to happen and was on his best behaviour. The other dogs took the whole thing more as if it were a fire-brigade display and made use of the opportunity to go round and settle minor differences.

The sportsmen were obviously very conscious of the importance of the occasion. Each came in his own peculiar full war-paint.

Tramp's master, a young farmer, came in riding boots and greatcoat. He had a broad, well-filled cartridge-belt like a strap round his stomach, and over his shoulder an old heirloom—a dark-stocked, gleaming-barrelled, heavy gun.

Kasper's master—or more correctly, leader, for Kasper was yard dog to a widow—hardly cut so fine a figure. He wore a cap and jacket and trousers, which were tied fast round his ankles and stuck into an enormous pair of short-legged boots with wooden soles, which made a great noise when he walked. Every moment he was peering and blowing down his cheap gun, which was so rusty that he had to use his knees when he wanted to shut it.

Both of these gentlemen had hunting pouches, but the little smallholder from the marsh—Lyn's breeder and trainer—who came in his blue working clothes, had provided himself with a sack. It hung loose over his shoulders and was, of course, to be filled with hares.

The sportsmen from the country town were naturally more elegantly dressed. The cattle dealer alone came in a stiff hat and a long brown mackintosh. He carried nothing but his gun and declared that pockets were best for carrying game. The tailor appeared with a rucksack which he had got from a big-game hunter, and which would hold a whole roebuck. When he unpacked a brand-new gun, it awakened astonishment in all, for it had three barrels and no cock.

"That thing's a great killer, isn't it?" asked the wild hunter from the great marsh. "Why, it ought to kill a hare from here to the ploughlands!"

Finally there were Kora's and Fille's owners. There was old Tyrbag, who for his part had come chiefly for the sight. He looked upon shooting as idling and instead of a gun he had a strong knotted stick in his hand. With that he would break Reynard's head, if by chance he visited one of his hen-runs. He had long since threatened to stand out of the annual shoot; but when he was told that Fille's capabilities as a hunting dog were mostly dependent on her master being with her, he hadn't the heart to carry out his threat.

Nobody attracted so much attention as Snapper's master. Nobody was so distinctively dressed or in such a peculiar style; but it was even more his dog which drew all eyes to him.

For this particular occasion the dog had been furnished with a muzzle, though this didn't seem to bother him much. In ecstasy at being set free from his kennel for the day he went about dragging his master after him by his heavy chain. The chain was on Snapper but the man held its end—and he was dragged along wherever Snapper wanted to go.

The meet broke up and the sportsmen proceeded into the fields in a long, close line.

He sat among the turnips, a little, silly beast, delighted, nay, intoxicated, with life. But now here came the hunters in a body, with long fire-tubes and dogs. They were out for sport, these honest, decent folk, who now, for the day, had armed themselves with guns; all of them felt themselves to be sportsmen by vocation, all of them were armed to the teeth and blazed away at every little partridge and hare that came their way.

Down they came in close ranks to the turnips. A partridge chick that flew up fell to the first shot five yards from the nearest sportsman; but before it reached the earth five other shots cracked, the hunters had plenty of powder.

They passed through the turnip field and entered a stubble field, into which Josse had escaped. He sat in the remains of a field-drain which even so late in the year still survived, crouched down among late-flowering, scentless camomiles and long, creeping blackberry branches.

They came straight towards him, and the dogs were busy. Little sharp-nose Fille, whose zeal he knew so well, passed close by him hunting a lark.

This gave Josse a shock, and as soon as the dog was past, he shot out so suddenly that he had leaped before the chorus of shots behind him began.

But Hopsy, who sat behind a hedge not far off, stayed still; and that was her doom. For the enemies were many and they came on in serried ranks.

She crouched in the grass, trusting with a touching intensity to that earth to which she had meant some day to entrust her leverets. And the earth covered her so well that her hunters were close on her before a boy shouted:

"Hi! There's a sitting hare!"

If she had sprung then, she would have had a chance; but she kept on trusting, for up to the present time that confidence of hers had never betrayed her.

The tailor, who knew how to approach a sitting hare, told the boy to be quiet and to get out of the way. He himself kept going round and round Hopsy in ever lessening circles. At last he put his gun to his shoulder and fired.

"There, that's how we shoot hares to-day," he cried, coming triumphantly over to the parish holding up a dead Hopsy by one back leg.

The parish clerk came up.

"You ought to be ashamed of yourself," said he. "You have murdered a hare in its form!"

But this outburst of the envious sportsman made no impression upon the tailor.

"It will taste none the worse for that," said he.

In the meantime Josse was leaping forward with the whole Bjaerg pack after him.

Lyn, the only one of the dogs which had not been freed, broke his leash when he laids eyes on the little runner's brown body, and started off with his long, arched leaps, his tail whipping his hocks and flanks. He was mute while he hunted, but he had what the other dogs lacked: a fine nose and temperament.

As to baying, there was no lack of it, for Josse was crossing the bare, stubble fields in full view of every dog.

Kasper hailed him the first. He ran with deep, slow barks that seemed to be dragged out one by one from his throat and then suddenly to break from it with great force; a moment later Fille struck up. Shrilly and passionately sounded the cur's little angry squeals. Then the rest of the Bjaerg choir joined in a loud, discordant chorus.

Every dog had its eye on Josse's coat and on his bobbing tail, and kept after him as persistently as the men who followed them. What kind of an animal he was only Lyn, whose flaming coat was foremost in the field, together with Kasper and Snapper, had the slightest idea. All the others took him for a rat, mole, hen robber or cabbage thief, who aroused all their inborn vigilance as guards, or their love of the chase as sporting dogs.

From the moment when Josse felt convinced that he must leave his form, he had his plan of flight arranged. He would either go up to the fence or down to the ditch. Which it should be depended upon the dogs, for he always sprang away from the place where they happened to be. Then he would go round Bjaerg, making a big arc to one side of it or the other.

But it would have to be by way of the ditch. He liked détours, for they checked the dogs.

Yes, he must go by the ditch and then towards the enclosed fields. He must go on to the willow-hedge, at the lower end of which, far out, was a new turnip field where he could take refuge and rest awhile. Lightly and elastically his paws touched the earth; he flew forward.

When he approached the refuge behind the line of willows, he made his first feint. It was simple and clumsy, he knew; he turned sharply and continued in the new direction instead of running straight on along by the hedge. Thus he at once got out of the line of sight of his pursuers, so that Tramp and the others, who hunted by their eyes, hesitated and gave up. But those dogs which followed by scent came on all the more eagerly.

Lyn was the foremost; but close at his heels came Kasper, Fille and Snapper. Snapper had long since rid himself of his muzzle. It had been made for his predecessor in the post of chained yard dog, a bulldog with a gigantic head. Snapper had never felt himself so free.

They dashed on along the hedge with foam at the corners of their mouths and swinging tails. Their noses were on the earth and they sniffed in Josse's scent.

Up to now Josse's heart had beat no faster than usual. Now he heard the baying of several more dogs than he had expected: still, he knew what dogs they were.

At full speed he came out from the hedge and went away across the hills. On the other side of the hills was a turnip field were the turnips no longer grew close together, so that his paws had a free course and the rustling of the leaves didn't hinder him from hearing.

Among the hills he met Girik and his mate, who with eleven chicks about them were lying and bathing in the sun-dried sand. They were having such a fine, peaceful time. For a moment Josse let peace enfold him too. His leap changed to a hop; then he sat down. His flanks were working, his nostrils quivering. With little, frightened squeaks the partridges separated. Then they gathered again in a group. They scraped the earth under them and lay down sideways.

Lyn, who was already far in front of the other dogs, came upon them like a squall of wind. The fluttered up and dispersed. Then Girik gave the assembly signal and drew his long flock of chicks clustered around him. Lyn tore madly after them for some distance.

Josse had reckoned aright when he lay down to rest among them.

But it wasn't long before he had Lyn back again and now the dogs began to prowl up and down among the turnips. Soon Kasper, too, came up on Snapper's very heels, and for the second time little Josse had to make off.

He scampered out of one end of a row as the baying dogs made their first leap into the other. The brief rest which Girik had afforded him had very much refreshed him. In the open field he leaped, full of jubilant spirits, high up into the air. He even made a sportive series of exultant leaps far out to the side. Soon the wildly baying chorus was left behind him. Only now and then, when he allowed himself too much leeway, standing up on his toes or making loops on his tracks, did he hear laboured breathing and the quick patter of paws behind him. He must get rid of that dog at the first opportunity. His road was almost a circle with the church as centre. Its circumference was a couple of miles. Josse thought it a fairly long turn to go round Bjaerg once. The lime pits, the pond, the mound, and the marsh were some of the milestones on the road round, which, like other roads, had its crossroads and corners, its hiding-holes and resting-places.

Meanwhile Lyn was gaining on Josse. Here in the open fields where the only refuge was the distant hills, Josse couldn't really get away. The scourge of hares had too easy a game to play, for at almost every moment Josse's brown body was before his eyes and so he could often take a good short cut.

They had now run pretty well half-way round Bjaerg and were far beyond the pond and the lime pits, rapidly nearing the marsh, when Josse suddenly had an idea.

The old rascal with the peculiarly sharp ears, that had so often gone for him when they had met by chance, was most likely in the ploughed fields on the other side of the marl hill. Josse had seen him preparing his bed there in the morning. The old fellow was irritable and suffered nobody near him. If one merely set foot in his field he used to spring up. He would risk it. Once before he had got the old rascal into hot water: that time he had done it just for fun, but now unfortunately he really had to.

Father Lepidus was lying in a deep furrow in a slight hollow in the earth which his big hind quarters completely filled. He had placed himself with his nose to the wind so that it shouldn't keep blowing away the warmth from under his coat. The crafty old fellow was sound asleep, but he heard every noise and distinguished them perfectly one from the other.

A moment since there had been Kasper's bay and Snapper's hoarse bark. He thought it strange that Snapper was loose, but made light of it. The dogs were a long way off anyhow!

Now he heard another kind of noise! This time he was shaken awake. He heard the pattering of paws, hare's paws—and close behind the pattering, the hard sound of a dog's paws smacking the earth. He raised himself slightly.

Oh, it was he, was it, the long-legged loper of Bjaerg? Beware of him, keep your eye on him; but he can easily be tricked!

The loper came into the ploughed field with Josse in front of him. Then Lepidus leapt. He had already waited longer than usual. He was unlucky enough to bob up just behind Josse—and he was a big hare. Lyn changed over—and went for *him*. The wild hunt went on over the fields, to a hollow lane, to the marsh and the far-off valley of the river. But Josse, satisfied that his trick had succeeded, made haste to settle himself in Father Lepidus's warm bed, where with relaxed muscles and galloping pulses he lay and gathered strength for a new effort.

The shouting, banging line of sportsmen was far away, but he hadn't to wait long for the main body of the four-legged pack. More and more clearly Josse heard Kasper's stormy barking, and took counsel of his paws as to whether or not he should take the risk and remain where he was. Meanwhile there was something about the canine chorus that struck him particularly. He missed one voice and it seemed to him that it was the high, squeaky treble. Perhaps he had been lucky enough to get rid of yet another pursuer, to lose Fille?

Yes, Fille hadn't been able to resist the turnip field, so full of various scents, into which Josse had led her. The shrewd little cur thought there was something suspicious about the whole affair: no mole had ever led her such a race before! So she resolutely broke away from the pack.

Josse stayed a little longer in his father's bed, and when at last he started out from it, he ran straight into the jaws of a baying hound!

With one leap he was across the ploughed field and another took him over a fence. There in the pasture land he came upon a number of ewes with their lambs. Josse made in among the sheep, which began in their terror to bleat and bob up and down in their thick fleeces.

Snapper was wild with excitement. Josse, whose long

ears were laid close along his back, disappeared before his nose in the grass with a couple of lambs in his wake.

Snapper's mouth watered furiously. He must catch something; he must bite something. He smelt hare distinctly where the hindmost lamb set its left foot. He approached the foot, his nose was tickled by wool, he opened his jaws, caught one of the lamb's hind legs, and tumbled it over and over to the edge of a water-hole.

This was a substantial hare he had caught hold of! Partridges which he ought to bring to his master slipped by him. He would have a hare to-day or die. He and the lamb rolled over the edge and into the water. And there Snapper did what, in his excited state of mind, he deemed to be his duty.

He was still enjoying himself to the top of his bent when a sportsman dripping with sweat, whistling and scolding, at last came up.

"Snapper!" shouted the man. "Snapper! Plague take the dog!"

But Snapper looked at him scornfully. He didn't understand how any man could fail to comprehend the field wildness of a poor yard dog let loose from its chain!

Once again Josse's guile had won him a small triumph and had successfully rid him of another pursuer. He had never seen Snapper, only heard him in the lonely nights; but he had judged him rightly by his voice. He was ferocious and ungovernable.

But Josse wasn't safe. Kasper kept on after him and Kasper was so accustomed to cows and lambs that they didn't confuse him in the least. *He* would never bite a sheep instead of a hare. He went on conscientiously after Josse: *this* rascal he was sure of; he must eat him!

Josse slowed down to half his usual speed. The reserve strength which had enabled him to get clear with a great forward leap each time Kasper came up with him was nearly spent. He couldn't manage to keep sufficiently in front to set one of his insoluble riddles. His previous brisk, regular gallop had become a mere scamper. Still he was running with all his might.

On his second round of Bjaerg he heard bawling and shooting in the distance. He rose for a moment on his hind legs to see his way. In front he heard Tramp's deep, gurgling bark; behind him came Kasper's now hoarse bay. He must go off his course; he must turn aside. "Now, paws, it's a matter of life and death!"

He ran along a boundary dike, the one he knew better than any other. It led to the ruins of the old house and to the safety of the blackthorn bush. Ah, it was only now, when he was nearing the place, that he remembered! The bush was gone! He must go through the elderwood, which was now thin and frozen, and in under the huge dancing-stone. The weasel lived there no longer, that he knew. She was touring the whole district with her growing children. He had met them in the marsh and in the lime pits, amid the remains of a wall in the churchyard and beyond the chambered barrow in the big mound. He need not worry; he would have the whole long-corridored dwelling to himself.

Through one of the many gaping fissures he slipped in and hid himself so deeply that he was in almost pitch darkness. There he sat and listened to his heart hammering against the cold stone that in a strange way seemed to echo its beating.

Kasper came up and began to run around the heap of

stones; but as he could find no exit he was sure that the rascal hare was inside. So he began to howl and bay and bellow at the top of his voice.

The line of sportsmen made its way across the field. Game birds and hares fell before them. Girik once again lost several of his chicks, and the large Lepidus family lost both young and old members. At last they came to the turnips where Fille was carrying on a continuous but not very profitable hunt, all by herself.

"Oh, here's Fille! Here's Fille!" cried the hunters joyfully. They were anxious to have news of the pack, which had been absent so long.

"Is Fille here?"

"Yes."

"Then come along, there must be game," cried the tailor, and hunted around with increasing eagerness.

Just at the end of a row of turnips he nearly trod on a hare. That was a fine fellow! Fille had started it and was hunting it round and round the sportsmen's very legs. The lust of the chase was at its height; everyone had his gun at his shoulder and was aiming at the animal as it was glimpsed now and then. Luckily nobody was shot; but when the guns banged, a howl was heard from poor Fille, who turned head over heels behind the unharmed hare and lay weltering in her blood.

In this wretched way did Josse's first little teacher depart this life. Jens Tyrbag was so angry that he refused to stay any longer—and this resulted in the disbanding of the parish shooting-party.

When the tailor was on his way home, he heard Kasper baying in the distance. The baying came from the ruins of the shepherd's house, the garden and surroundings of which had just been thoroughly gone through. But the tailor was so mad on shooting that he went there alone. He was very curious as to what it might be that Kasper was baying about. Was he baying at a cat? No, a yard dog like Kasper wouldn't hunt cats.

When he came to the heap of stones he began at once, led by the dog's eager nose, to break his way in to Josse. He pulled off his coat and worked like a black, throwing big and little stones round about him.

Josse backed deeper and deeper into his refuge. But however slender and pliant he made himself, however low he crouched, he couldn't move a hand's breadth further. Outside the stone heap was the tailor. He threw the lumps of stone about so that the whole place was filled with the noise. And now from this side and now from that came the pattering of diligent paws. Ah, it wasn't Josse now, but someone else, that was playing on the dancing-stone!

All at once the moist, black gristle of the dog's nose was stuck through a little fissure in the thick ceiling over Josse's head. He gave it a good, hearty smack; he snorted at it and slapped out with his paws. But that only made the dog more and more furious and he began to growl and bark. A pair of hands carefully lifted the big stone that covered Josse's hind quarters. A pair of man's eyes peeped cautiously in.

"Ha, ha, a hare! . . . Yes, indeed, there he sits!" The tailor had a sudden inspiration.

"Let's catch it alive. That'd be something new! . . ."

He took off the strap of his gun and fastened it round Kasper's neck. The unruly dog might get in his way. A moment later Kasper found himself tied to a tree.

Then the tailor carefully raised the stone, slid his arm

in over Josse, caught hold of his long ears and hauled him out.

Josse uttered several muffled hisses, and, while his back kept bending and straightening itself, he brought the sharp, outstretched claws of his powerful back legs up over his head and in doing so was lucky enough to scratch his persecutor quitely deeply on the arm. Josse had never been in such a scrape as this and he kicked so hard that the tailor, in order to keep hold of him, had to hold him pressed close against his chest. With one hand he held him by the ears, with the other he tried to control Josse's hind quarters. But Josse tore the buttons off his waistcoat, even clawed his shirt and nearly got through to his skin.

Involuntarily the tailor bent and tried to get Josse as it were into a vice between his knee and his chest. But Josse met violence with violence! He made long gashes in the tailor's hands, and just as the latter thought he had got hold of him properly and bent his head to take a look at his captive, Josse kicked up so fiercely that he fixed his black claws into the tailor's face.

The gash he made there checked his foe: his nose was bleeding; he had to take one hand off Josse to catch hold of it; and when he brought his hand down again and saw it covered with blood—his own blood—he got a shock and loosened his grip.

In a moment Josse, slippery as an eel, broke free from his captor and, despite Kasper's wildest protests and to the unlucky tailor's great amazement, was quickly out of sight of both the tailor and his dog.

CHAPTER XII

A NOVEMBER NIGHT

JOSSE'S kingdom was now ploughland—field after
field of black earth—but his November form, deep
down among the grassy clods that the plough had
turned over, was as good as any house.

The nights got darker and darker.

He had to leave his form early in the evening in order
to scrape up as much food as possible. There was but
an hour and then darkness descended upon the earth
and swallowed up the tender shoots of the green rye
and young clover.

Still his eyes could discern yellow, withered stems and
follow the ditch in which they grew down through the
fields. He still saw clearly the willows by the boundary
dike and the few isolated thorn-bushes persisting here
and there by dike and path that were his landmarks.

But the darkness grew ever thicker about him; it came like a black mist up from the earth and piled one layer upon another; it closed him in like a snowdrift.

The cold, rainy days had long ago banished the cows from the fields and the calves and bulls were also at home in their stalls. No animal now saluted him with neighing or bellowing when he left his form for food in the evening, and there was no comfortable chewing to be heard in the clover when he was returning home in the morning. It grew more and more quiet out in the open field. Indeed, he began to long a little for company.

Where were the little hares he used to meet? Lab, with whom he had once played puss-in-the-corner, he couldn't even remember. He had only been a leveret when Lab had been there and everything was so new and rushed in on him so confusedly that nothing fixed itself rightly in his brain. But he had come to know Hopsy and that crafty old hare, his father, and many another, who on quiet evenings or merry mornings had gambolled joyously with him.

The first evening he came to Jens Tyrbag's green rye and did not find, as usual, a yellowish-grey hare sitting and chewing, all hunched up, with her ears along her back, he had a strange impression. Hopsy had never been a vagabond like himself. He had always come upon her just in that same hollow; she had almost been one of his landmarks.

Nor were there dogs to be seen now. Bjaerg's proud pack was safe at home and many of its best members were doing their proper work.

Josse's mother had happened to be the cause of Fille's death. Snapper, the sheep thief, now sat chained in his kennel and howled. The "Scourge to Hares" was gone too—for a long time and perhaps for ever he was out of the game. Father Lepidus, who knew how to deal with pursuers of his type, had given him his deserts. He had been found behind a big stone lying stiff and stark and unable to move. The vets couldn't promise that he would ever be the same dog again. The farmhands, who knew Lyn so well, expressed the prevailing opinion in the profound sentence: "He must have bitten off more than he could chew."

Josse became more and more eager to get nearer to Bjaerg.

He had often been on his way to repeat the visit he had paid it in the summer, but a dog or a cat had always got in his way. The lovely perfume of the gardens, full of such good things as fruit-trees and spicy herbs, remained unimpaired. Many a night, when the fields lay bare and his favourite plants had withered away, the spicy herb beds of Bjaerg came back into his mind. What if he tried his luck there once more?

One night Josse, alone in his kingdom, sat behind a wind-beaten willow tree.

The wind hissed and raved through the willow and piped and whistled among its thin twigs. It whipped and tore at his woolly coat and shook his long, black-tipped ear-lobes about.

When the rain drove down in a swift stream, Josse had to make as much haste as he could, crouch his long, concertina-like body together, and ride out the deluge in a furrow. The storm swept over his head and tore at the roots of the grass. Showers came pouring down with a sound like pattering paws and with cold, lashing drops. Water ran down the furrow and collected in Josse's form. He had to get up and shake his coat every minute.

The big showers were followed by a drizzle which he got in his face, so that he sneezed and had to wipe his muzzle carefully. He got up out of the furrow, hopped off, and settled himself in a nook behind his dear mound. There he was tolerably comfortable, sitting and listening to his three big, humming trees communing with the weather. The rain worked down to their very roots, so that the earth simply quivered under them.

The clouds looked blacker and blacker as if the night was annoyed at his keeping good-tempered in this comfortless darkness!

These were hard times for Josse. There was nothing in the fields that he could get his teeth into. Three or four times he had eaten the fallen yellow leaves of the aspen.

Again Bjaerg's spicy scents and vegetable-gardens came into his mind. In weather like this one could do with a little cabbage in one's stomach!

So he set forth.

He couldn't find the little crooked path by which as a leveret, in the summer, he had slipped in. If he wanted to go Bjaerg, he would have to follow the big, broad high road, which went in at one side of it and out at the other.

He was eyeing it already, hopping slowly forward. He would see. In the darkness of night Bjaerg looked like an immense mound before him, and the church-tower and the whitewash on the houses gleamed.

He stood still and moved his ears backwards and forwards, testing every gust of wind from Bjaerg with his long funnel-like ears, breathing in and sniffing the air that came to him down the road. But he noticed nothing suspicious about it.

"Courage!" Josse went forward along the road into Bjaerg.

In among the men's dwellings it was even darker than out in the open fields. The great blocks of stone, the long, high fences, the big, old trees, in comparison with which he, even if he stood right up on his toes, felt like an atom! All these things seemed to collect the darkness about them and to draw the storm gradually to them.

The familiar, monotonous blowing with which the wind of the fields often entertained his ears for days together was not what one heard here. Here the wind howled and bellowed from every side and there was a regular Babel of sound.

Overwhelmed by the violence of the storm, Josse stopped and sat undecided for a moment there on the road. He spoke in dumb show with the storm and discovered by degrees that he could hear twice as clearly here and could distinguish the chewing of the cattle in the nearest cow-shed and the snoring of a chained dog in his kennel. With a sudden brisk leap he moved away from the nearest blocks of stone and turned into the road that led past the village pond down along by the enclosed fields where the calves were kept.

There it was muddy, slushy and wet. In the air which came to him he smelt all those queer mingled odours which he remembered from his first visit. Suddenly he sniffed at something which he thought he ought to know. It was his big burdock from the border dike, under which he and Lab had once taken shelter and which he had often longed for. Look, here it was, but not in the guise in which he had seen it then. It was standing on its head with its root in the air and was resting its flabby, dry leaves and shrivelled stems on its big, thick, rounded burrs.

Beside it in the same heap he came upon all the plants of the dike and the meadow and the field, lying dry and withered, stem by stem, and he drew them towards him, recognizing them by their scent. Here they were all garnered in! He hopped curiously round them and found blackthorn branches and the hawthorn in which he had escaped from the weasel. They lay in heaps, dry and withered, smelling strongly like everything else. And the great stone, the strange humpy body of which he knew so well in the field, here it was, too!

But when on his way he came near the first regular hill he stood up on his paws. Now he caught again, more strongly and sharply than he had ever caught it in the fields, the real, genuine odour of the farmhands.

At every second or third leap he heard a sound that made him stop and listen. Now a cock crowed, ending up with a deep "Gok, gok"—Josse knew him. It was the cock that lived in the farm out by the marsh. Now geese cackled in a pen, and there was a lonely mournful voice from the other end of the village. That was a gander. Josse knew that too. Since the late autumn had come it had cried "Yah, yah" like this, and then sighed deeply and sorrowfully as an equinoctial storm sighs among the hills and in sedge and reeds. The men had slaughtered his own goose—his wife to whom he had been married for two years!

Josse was on his way to the delicious cabbages and the spicy smell of the parsley was already in his nose. He investigated the road and the gardens and listened to every snore in the whole village. Everything was quiet—quiet in spite of the chaos and the noise.

He squeezed through a thorn hedge into the cabbages.

He chose out the freshest leaves. He knew how to get those that were the crispest and greenest and most luscious and leave those that were yellow and withered alone. From time to time he stopped his chewing and sniffed and watched on every side—everything was quiet except the chaos of the storm. Everything was as it usually was at night.

Meanwhile, when the breaks in the clouds became considerable and the earth stretched all about him fully lit up, when he perceived the shadows of his own whiskers and of his long ears, and the white moon fixed its eye upon him, he felt strangely unsafe and anxious. Then he felt a deep, irresistible longing for the fields, where he had a free road. He must go, out through the hedge and away down to the road. His hunger was appeased; he was full to bursting. Why should he stay here among the howling blocks of stone? No, he must away, away! past the chewing cows and the snoring watch dog, past Kasper's farm and Jens Tyrbag's water-tower—out to the fields where the storm's voice in his ears did not sound like sighs or weeping, but was a deep, rushing roar like the most beautiful music.

Many a visit did Josse pay to the village. Hunger drove him there when in the darkness of the night he sat in the field and Bjaerg's delicious dainties came into his mind.

Each whiff through lattice-work, each vegetable-shed where cabbage and celery were stored, each stackyard that offered him a taste of oats, he came to know. The dogs could yelp and bay at him—what did he care for that! The cats could mew and howl most dismally—it didn't worry him in the least. He knew the superiority of his paws and of his senses. Without even pricking up his ears he went on with his meal.

He often met Lepidus, the old crafty hare, on his expeditions. Once on a white, moonlit night when he was sitting on Jens Tyrbag's lawn and talking in dumb show to his own shadow, another shadow glided suddenly out from somewhere by his side, and it had an extraordinarily pointed nose and mean, crafty ears. He trembled feverishly, even as he took the mighty leap which landed him far away out of the old one's sight.

But besides the cat, one of the farmhands sometimes lay in wait for him on moonlight nights. Many hares were shot; but Josse never happened on a place where there were watchful eyes and good guns. He visited places where a dozing servant lad sat with a rusty blunderbuss which he couldn't fire, or he transferred the danger to some cat that was out prowling.

Neither men nor dogs ever caught him.

CHAPTER XIII

THE DEATH OF LEPIDUS

WINTER was knocking at the door.

From the east came the great, snow-laden cloud-masses, distinguishable from the autumn rain-clouds by their bluish gleam. The pools were frozen and the black mole-hills in the meadows and ploughed fields shone with a white, glittering surface. The telephone wires sang wildly and shrilly, while from the sombre, heavily-clouded horizon one torn cloud after another swept upwards.

Josse was weather-sick and had been so for many days. He still had an unpleasant, empty rumbling in his stomach. His fine senses had already announced the coming of the snow. He was sitting at the edge of the marl-hill in a form between the grey willows and scrub.

The storm blew his whiskers down on to his chin; the wind whirled round his flanks and through the hair on his back. The snowflakes fell more thickly like a swarm of gnats which stung and pricked him, slapping hard and wet against his face. They made the storm visible, and thronged the air as though they were living creatures.

He shook himself and pressed back almost to the bottom of his leaf-lined lair to escape the snow.

But the flakes fumed and hissed in his face and, falling close to the place where he sat, heaped themselves up around him. Soon his sides were covered, then his thighs. Now the flakes were eating up his head, his neck, his ears; now they were covering his arched back. The snowstorm was burying him.

The snow wasn't slushy or damp. It was drift, fine and white like flour. The storm whirled whole clouds of it round at a time and flung them with all the might of its clenched fist upon the earth.

The storm was outside. The mouse had its hole, the owl its nest, the crow its refuge in the hospitable wood. The fox had its hole and the weasel its heap of stones. But what had Josse?

Josse had his peace of mind, his patience, his good humour—and his thick, woolly coat. He understood what made life happy; to dwell in the present and to give oneself completely into the power of the passing moment. He didn't long for the spring, he didn't sigh for the summer; he took what life offered him of sorrow and delight day by day; even under the drift and in the snowstorm!

Late in the morning the storm abated. Josse stuck his head out of the air hole in his snow hut. Everything that he saw was white, white, white . . . glittering, blinding white. He didn't recognize his fields. Bjaerg and the highest stone on the top of the church-tower were gone. Only a kind of heap of rime-covered brush-wood was to be seen. Where were the grey willows that had stood behind his lair and the long, quivering, withered grass he had had straight before him in the hollow? And where was the little trembling thorn?

The white rain had swallowed them all up!

He had to stand right up on his very tail and stay so for a long time and look about him. Yes, it emerged little by little. That white hill there was the solitary distant farm; and a little scrap of cloud that seemed to hang threateningly over the top of the hill on the horizon was just the top of the little thorn bush.

Just then he cast a glance round for the trees. He was so familiar with them, so sure he would recognize them! Weren't they one of his landmarks, those "humpy elms"? They marked the crossways where the field path crossed the high road. Soon Bjaerg's stone heaps emerged under their snow-covered roofs; he could make out the tree trunks in their gardens and over there were the mill and the church tower, both rising above the white mass.

But it wasn't *home* to him. It was as though he had come into a strange land; his fields and meadows, his clover-perfume, and the still surviving turnip tops were all gone.

He left his form and began to wander over the snow. It was soft to walk on, but heavy to hop on. He fol-lowed the dips in the earth to which he was accustomed and came to a hedge which led him farther over the fields. Then he came down to his birthplace, the old lime pit, the sheltered spot in which he had been born

and which had been made unrecognizable by the snow.
Only the stiff stems of the seeded wild chervil still jutted
up. When he sniffed them and rubbed his chin against
them he felt that now he was really at home.

Everywhere he saw mice slipping about. The snow
forced them to come up and show their brown, plump
bodies. A little later, as he was hopping across the highway, he came upon a whole assembly of mice round
some horse-droppings!

Near the end of the lime pits he heard the old wind-
motor snoring and so found the trench that brought
water through the fields. Now he guessed where one of
his pantries lay. That was right! There was the little
willow-copse sticking up out of the snow near the pond,
and there was ice, thick and yellow, coating the lapwings' meadow. He just had to skip over the trench and
there should be oat-stubble and young clover there.

He came across Girik and his starving little flock
running about aimlessly unable to get their bearings.
Each partridge was looking out for itself. They were
scraping valiantly to keep themselves warm. But of corn
in their crops there was none.

Girik had no sense of locality. He, who had so often
helped Josse, had now to be helped by him. Josse was
able to show the partridges the way to the rye field and
the young clover. He could also scrape deep holes down
to the food, and into these the partridges gratefully
dived.

They now came together to the *lazy farmer's* fields.
On these lay heap after heap of oats raked together;
trampled down and half mouldy to be sure, but still
edible. And the birds and Josse blessed this poor man-
creature, who had not yet gathered his harvest in. His
hunger meant their feeding! Josse found one of the

biggest heaps and at once began scraping. So did the yellowhammers, goldfinches and siskins; while Girik and his wife took their places at the table when it was laid.

When Josse had shown them the way to do it and scraped away the top covering of snow, Girik could look after the rest. With great delight he raked and scraped to right and left.

But Josse thought he knew of a better store. Just a few quick leaps away the Farmer Tyrbag had his turnip field. The turnips were gone, that Josse knew, but fortunately the green tops had been left behind.

It was owing to Josse's great experiences that, following the indications given him by his efficient little nose, he came to the exact place where deep under the snow lay the green, juicy leaves. They had already been gnawed, it was true, but they were still useful. If he had had to depend upon his eyes alone, things would scarcely have gone so well. They all shouted "turnips" when they saw the first little clod that rose up like a hump under the snow. Then the partridges came up again, following on his heels, and reaped the benefit of his find. So did Josse repay in the course of the day a great part of his debt to Girik.

Would the winter quite kill him?

He had endured a month's frost and cold before, one day, the wind seemed a little softer to his muzzle. Here and there his dear ploughland came into sight and his green rye too—but oh, how shrivelled and subdued it was! It had had a hard time too! But it was only for a short time that the milder wind blew; he soon felt fore-warnings of a change and the bite of the wind was like the bite of fox or dog. One snowstorm succeeded an-

other and the drift sometimes accumulated for days together.

There lay little Josse's fruitful land, white and cold,
in the grasp of winter: fields and meadows, pasture and
marsh were one white sheet. The dear rye, the hospitable clover, the faithful ditches with their store of
grass—all gone, without leaving a trace!

But nothing is so bad as to be hopeless. Later on the
snow became so hard that the drifts formed bridges
over thorn hedges and wire fences. At night Josse could
make his way unhindered all over the village gardens
and could even get inside the innermost fence within
which the curly-leafed cabbages lay. Right up to the
tops of the snowed-in fruit-trees, which up to the present time his teeth had never been able to gnaw, lay the
frozen drifts forming a strong rampart. Josse sat like a
bird in the tops of the trees and felt that winter was
endurable.

Another hare was crossing the snow-covered fields.
It didn't move lightly in brisk hops like Josse. It limped
and hobbled and dragged slowly onwards.

Once this hare, too, had moved swiftly over the top
of the rifts and in long, flying leaps had skimmed over
ploughland and meadow. None had excelled it is smelling out turnip leaves or digging through the snow to the
clover or winter grain.

But at last men had crippled it. At last men had been
able to rob it of its speed.

Lepidus had been damaged by shot amid the tempting
cabbage plots. The crafty old fellow, who in the course
of his frequent visits to the other side of the valley had
taken such toll of the owner's fruit that the owner had
set a price on his head, had at last met his fate.

The Death of Lepidus

He knew it quite well. His mind was suddenly filled with a fear he had never known before, and each time he heard a dog bark or a man approach, he felt terror quiver through his whole body. He, who had counted a fox as no more than a cat, simply shook when his sharp ears and nose brought news of the hereditary enemy of his race.

He was defenceless, as he knew well. He was completely at the mercy of all. He felt like a snail—he who in front of the farmers' pack had travelled with lightning speed and zigzagged, too, like forked lightning.

The damaged back leg itched and burned as if he had but that moment run through a clump of stinging nettles. If he touched the earth with it, it was as though the teeth of all the dogs and foxes in the world were tearing and flaying it. Wound-fever was fully developed and the inflammation sent its merciless itching pains through his bones. His leg was swollen to twice the size of the tailor's fist.

If the tailor who had shot him had only for an hour suffered a small part of what his poor victim had to endure for days and weeks, he would perhaps for the future have kept to his bed at nights. As it was, he only cursed his bad luck, and when in the morning he saw a lot of bloodstains on the snow, he comforted himself with the phrase: "The shot must have hit him, and that well, and he has had his deserts."

For five successive days after his wounding Lepidus lay quietly in a form which he had scraped in the snow in an open field behind a hill. He dared not take shelter behind a fence or hide himself in a warm place among the reeds of the marsh, for he knew that just there the fox was wont to walk at night. The hard frost pierced to his very bones and stiffened the injured limb. It was like a cooling bandage that eased the burning pain. He felt no hunger but only the thirst of fever, so that he had to keep continually swallowing snow.

One evening, in the twilight, he limped out with his long ears erect. He must be more than usually cautious. He would go to the green rye. At last he had felt the desire for a little food.

On the same evening the vixen slunk out of her den. She was so hungry that she could have eaten an earthworm greedily.

The winter sky with its white gleam of stars arched over her. Her whiskers froze and the frost touched her nose with its cold fingers. At each step the snow cracked under her paws.

Hedge and fence cast their black silhouettes on the snow and the shadows cast by the poplars at the wayside reached far over the white fields. Now and then a dark lump seemed to break away from the shadows and begin to roll away across the snow. That was a hare on its way to the turnip pits or to the patches of green rye.

The vixen stood still and curled her tail round her hind quarters and composed herself to observe the hares.

The Lepidus family were cowardly fellows, who never, like a rat or a cat, dared to defend themselves. They did nothing but run; they did nothing but use their legs to baulk her. She despised the hares, but nourished in the depths of her soul a secret admiration for them. For if she were to be quite honest with herself, she must admit that they excelled her in craftiness and speed.

It was therefore with particular delight that she made away with every leveret she met with. She ate them not only for the purpose of satisfying her hunger, or because they tasted so good—she ate them also because experience had taught her that if she didn't catch them while they were little, she would never catch them at all—and then later on she would have more tricksters to cause her annoyance.

Those hares, those hares! and in particular that old sly one with the big haunches, the rust-red hair on the shoulders, and the long sticks of legs, that had always been a thorn in her side! She could never go out by herself to hunt at night without that swift, sly old rascal finding her out. To whatever field she came all round Bjaerg—in the latest twilight or in the earliest dawn, in the stormy but moonlight nights that were so dear to her—she always found him before her or at her side. Like a black, ill-omened shadow he kept by her. If she went sniffing along a ditch he was sitting there, and he passed her by on the top of the hill; if she slunk into a hole in the marl she never failed to see *his* long, inquiring ears slip past in the darkness just in front of the place she had slunk out from. Sometimes, urged by hunger or driven by her duties as a mother, she ventured to go to the Bjaerg farms and see if she might be lucky enough to get a hen that had been locked out or a dead calf or sucking pig that had been thrown away. Then she could always be sure that in any garden, the thorn-hedge of which was open at the bottom, or through which there were "passages", she would catch a glimpse of the impudent, artful fellow.

What was *he* doing there in Bjaerg? *He* didn't eat blackbirds or dead sucking pigs. He was more afraid of dogs that she was and didn't dare to let even a kitten come near him! She wondered what he was doing when he sat and listened on the tops of hillocks or leaped round the marl hill, where she and her lawful progeny were hidden. Why was the cowardly leaper always anxious to see her go first into her day-shelter in the grain or clover, before he hid himself away as men appeared with the daylight?

She slunk on farther through the night.

A crescent moon shone obliquely in the sky. It had a large halo round it. From time to time there was a sharp, sudden quacking in the air above her. The wild ducks were making tracks for river and stream from more open water.

She sneaked along down by a hedge and up over a hill, and there she came suddenly upon a hare's tracks and from sheer habit followed them for a couple of leaps. Then she noticed that there was a smell of blood in those tracks. It became more and more distinct. Instinctively she developed a burning interest in that familiar series of four-fold tracks. All other prey was forgotten. The tracks held her attention for more than a mile—and now involuntarily she changed over from a trot to a gallop.

But Lepidus had heard the vixen coming long ago. He was in full flight, yet he knew quite well that he was moving far too slowly. Stems and blades of rough grass sticking up out of the snow that usually bent to his leap now stood up, stiff and pointed. The pain in his leg did not trouble him overmuch for the moment. He was much too occupied with trying to escape.

The ruins of the old house by which he limped were drifted over and looked like a great heap of snow. But round on its lee he found, among some gooseberry bushes, a tolerable refuge. The craving he had felt in his infancy to get away and lie in a dark place came over him with irresistible strength. He, this old villain of a hare that had driven the pack mad and had scattered it over there in the baron's shooting-grounds, crept into this refuge like a rabbit.

He hadn't sat there very long, enduring the frightful pains which now began to shoot with redoubled strength through his leg, when the vixen, led by the blood in the tracks, slipped round the ruins of the house and came upon him. The onslaught was so quick and so craftily carried out that Lepidus could only make a couple of pitiful leaps.

He had been hunted all his days and had had enemies perpetually threatening him. Still, he had never, even during the wildest chase, lost heart. Now suddenly he lost. His leg had betrayed him! For the first time in his life he gave in, complaining, sending out into the night shrill cries of distress, like the cries of a baby.

And the vixen shook and tortured him unmercifully. Lepidus kicked out and gashed the fox's toe with his sharp nails. His smooth woolly coat made it almost impossible for the vixen to get a grip. It was a long, long time before the vixen had done with the proud old rascal hare.

Then there emerged from a hole in the heap of snow a little slender, chalk-white animal with something like a beetle hanging from almost the tip of its tail. Attracted by the shrieks of the hare, the weasel came towards the spot and raised herself high on her forelegs, with her little head held up in the air at the end of her long neck. Her little coal-black eyes danced and her rat-like ears glistened eagerly. She heard Lepidus's last groan and saw the vixen stand sniffing before her.

Once a fox had cheated Jit-Jit of a hare; now, perhaps, she would get her own back! She must try to get her share of the banquet.

The vixen remembered that devil of a weasel quite well, and this time she was quite decided not to let herself be caught by the nose.

It came to a fight for the booty, as always happens when hungry beasts of prey meet.

The vixen caught Jit-Jit by the back of the neck and shook her thoroughly for several minutes. But when she flung the weasel from her it was still living. Jit-Jit wanted to try her old trick; but the fox was prepared. Jit-Jit consequently cast her whole head and front part of her body right into the vixen's jaws and a moment afterwards was dead.

CHAPTER XIV

THE LITTLE DOE HARE

THE earth was no longer white and hard; it was soft and greasy and it shone black. It hung from Josse's claws and stuck to his paws, so that he had to keep his legs straight and walk as if he were on stilts not to get his belly dirty. There was water in the furrows and rapid streams ran through the field-drains.

The air was very mild and the sun warmed him thoroughly. He sat grinning and bristling his whiskers.

There were clear pools of water among the clover; its green, fresh leaves projected from them. Josse saw himself reflected in them. Like wanton, singing jets of water released from icy bondage, the larks rose jubilant into the air. They were pert and playful and the cocks chased each other in fun.

The magpies were dragging sticks to the hedge. Their domed nest in the blackthorn tree was growing. It looked to Josse like a big black cat lying in wait in the tree!

He hopped down to the pond, while the lapwings swept in long, swinging curves over the meadows—each of them making a series of following billows before his eyes. Each time the birds rose and showed their white, shining bellies he saw the tops tipped with foam and the deep, greenish-black hollows between as they rushed downwards in a tumbling dive. He could also see their gleaming emerald backs and the upper side of their wings.

In the little gap in the marl, which had been so choked up with drifted snow before, the willows were already standing in slush, and in the drifts at the bottom of the slope he saw his snowstorm refuge-holes, gaping and earth-blackened like the entrances to deep pits. Cock yellowhammers twittered in the tops of the willows and their gray mates sat fascinated, listening to them.

Over the mound, where the tall aspen and the little wild bird-cherry trees crowded together, a flashing red kestrel fluttered in and out caressing the spring air with its pointed wings. The mound had been the first place where the snow melted, as though there were an inner warmth in the great knoll. Waterfalls streamed down its side, and in the drifted earth that remained behind when the snow disappeared, young spring grass and sprouting herbs were already peeping up.

Josse made many excursions; each time he came upon more and more partridges; they lay about in pairs. Girik was again paying court to his little wife. He had driven the children away, having divided the fields up between them. He was perturbed and uneasy, on tiptoe with excitement, for there was another cock, a cunning old fellow, who had attached himself to the flock during the winter and was doing his best to oust Girik. Morning and evening they fought, running about with wrathful eyes and flapping wings and crowing in competition.

But Mrs. Girik had no doubt which she preferred.

Josse was afoot early and late. There was something

of the explorer, of the wanderer in him. Starting from the tuft of grass on the edge of the clay mound, where he was born, he had gradually explored the whole of his native countryside, traversed it this way and that by night and by day, and had learned to know it to its farthest corners. From the pond in the southwest to the marsh in the northeast, on every side of the white tower on the hill, he knew the direction of every ditch and every fence; where there were roads and paths, and whither they led. He knew the dogs, he knew the cats, he knew the fox and the weasel and the crows and the falcon—and he knew men.

Now he was big and trained, and he no longer let himself be chased to a standstill.

Like his late father, old Lepidus, he began to hanker after what was far away. He had already acquired the habit of settling for his day's rest far beyond the outermost fields, and when at night he circled around Bjaerg and its big tower, he involuntarily made his circles larger and larger. Before, he could in all probability have done the whole round tour in half a night; but now he had made it so extensive that it took him many days.

He found it sad and lonely in the Bjaerg neighbourhood. The others of his kind had been either shot or driven away, and now he longed more than ever to rub noses with another hare.

When he ran about in the dawn it often seemed to him that he saw a hare sitting in the ploughed field or among the green rye. Then his heart rejoiced and his body longed to gambol, and he would approach in a leap a yard long, make a high hop of salutation and a dumb show with his ears while he slapped his stomach with his forepaws. But alas! when he sniffed at it, it was only a plump stone or a brown molehill.

The desire to wander, mighty and incalculable, grew in him. He must go out and meet other hares—he must go forth and subdue new meadows to himself. When the wind was in the west he often smelt the air full of the scent of spicy herbs and delicious things to eat, and he was involuntarily drawn in the direction whence it came—towards the river valley and the far-off woods.

It no longer froze at night. The pools had thawed. In them the stars were mirrored.

It was quiet, mild weather and, for Josse, as light as day. He went softly and noiselessly about the place. The top of the bordering dike and the billowing earth of the ploughed fields, the dry oat stubble and the green rye did not crack or groan under his paws. Big Kora slept no longer in the barn; she was out at night. She stood at the entrance to her farmstead, and now and then let her deep voice be heard—"Wuff, wuff"—and the dogs round about in Bjaerg replied. Joose recognized each by its bark.

Girik crowed from the dike amid the hills. Another little cock crowed longer. A third shrilled still longer. Then Josse felt he had to go.

Where he was going to he didn't know, but he hopped away, and as he went, he nibbled with a good appetite at the sprouting herbs of spring. Between mouthfuls he was overpoweringly conscious of a feeling of vitality and had to set forth over the fields at such speed that the dew was like a spring shower about his ears. In less than a second he could change from a sitting position into a lightning leap. At his wildest speed he could stop so suddenly that the long hairs on his back blew up backwards. He could run so that trees and tufts of grass seemed to run with him. He was the fleetest of foot in all the land.

They ought to have known what he thought of himself! He was conscious of his superiority of speed and the power of turning quicker than all that barking rabble. Folk thought him simple, without craftiness or discrimination. Perhaps that was why he was still there, though many would have liked to have him.

He hopped up on to an unplanted, grass-grown, bordering dike, rose on his hind legs as high as he could, and took one of his long surveys of the country round, far and wide.

Everything his eyes found lovely and his paws worthwhile he found in his kingdom. There were fields and meadows, marshes and ponds, little gleaming lakes and high-domed hills, hedges and dikes, and over yonder, big, dreaming woods. At times the air hung heavy and dark over this native countryside of his. But it could also delight his soul with the play of warm, glittering sunrays.

The night was full of the lapwings' cry. The birds were calling all about him. They were cheeky and playful. The billowing of their wings never ceased and in the grass at his feet lay the mice. There was a peculiar restlessness in the air. There was whirl after whirl above his head. He heard strange sounds coming from the moving birds: whistling and calling, screeching and trumpeting—all were on the wing.

The darkness grew thicker. The calling of the hens ceased. For a moment there was a great, deep stillness. A solitary light winked in a farmhouse window.

Unfortunately for Josse he hopped from the dike out into the highway just as a big, fiery-eyed monster leaped forward. Josse at once fell into his usual hop, with all

kinds of fun in his head and all kinds of mad gambols
tingling in his legs. Then the motor bellowed with sup-
pressed fury like the big bull in the fields.

Josse hadn't time to make one of his side-springs. He
just had to travel like an express train. He was very
confused. His little brain, his whole jolly little soul, were
centred as usual down in his saving legs.

Every fibre in his body asked which way the paws
wanted to go. His paws wanted to go where the road
was the evenest, where there were no hindrances in the
way, where they could get up the greatest speed—those
good, ever dutiful paws!

So they went on out into the road, right in front of
the car. His paws didn't hesitate, of course not—he had
never doubted them. He noticed that he was shooting
away from the danger—that the monster couldn't com-
pete with him. He had a mind to fling his legs out backwards both to right and left, to scurry from one side of
the road to the other, mocking his pursuer, or, still
speeding along, to talk to him in dumb show.

But the car was in a hurry—it soon informed the paws
that they had never had its equal for speed behind them.
And the paws saw the track before them, bordered by
grass and heaps of broken stones, turnings and many
other obstacles that would hinder their speed if they
came up against them. So they kept faithfully to the
middle. Gradually they ceased to play tricks and ran on
at their greatest possible speed.

Stupid paws! They should have sacrificed a second,
moderated their speed, and sprung aside over the ditch;
but now they dared not delay for anything. For a very
long way Josse kept on in front of the car.

But the bellowing monster kept on gaining on him
and the moment came when the agile paws confided to

him anxiously that they could do no more. Then Josse's head swam. He lost his presence of mind. And the paws told him it was all over with him.

The car was nearly upon him. The light from its lamps streamed blindingly over him. It was catching up with the swiftest runner in the land. He flung himself with a sudden flop down on the road and stiffened into a clod. The paws had failed him for the first time in his life—perhaps the earth would help.

It did. . . .

Snorting loudly the car passed over him, while he crouched down between the noiseless wheels. Like a will-less, new-born creature he sat up—uncomprehending but unharmed.

Terror left him. He saw again the surrounding trees and plants; he saw a yellow coltsfoot and a clump of St. John's wort dried up by the winter. He heard the lapwings call and the monster driving away into the distance. But wasn't he hurt? Something sticky, something wet, was dripping down his chin. He let it go on down to his tongue, and the tongue licked his chin and got something acrid, oily and greasy on it. It was nothing belonging to *him*, of that he was sure. There was something about it that passed his understanding and had to do with horse and cow and dog and man.

He carefully stroked one ear and then the other. He tried straightening his back. Yes! That was all right. Intoxicated with happiness, he got up. Could he move his legs? Could he leap? Yes! That was all right too! He could do both. Then he became wild. He shook the dust from him and raced away over the fields. Then he sat down in a comfortable place and began to caress those delicate paws of his, those dear victorious little paws.

He saw that he had come a long, long way. When he took his bearings, he noticed that he knew none of the ditches or hedges and that he was in new fields and strange meadows full of hare-tracks.

One of the tracks impressed him particularly. He couldn't sit still long. He had to be up and moving with his nose close to the earth. Leaping and rushing, he raced over field after field and the longer he kept on the track the wilder and more intoxicated he felt. He sped across ploughed field after ploughed field without even noticing one of the furrows. He passed over wheat and rye without so much as looking at the fresh, sappy, bluish-green leaves. An ever increasing rush of life possessed him and he gave himself wholly up to it.

At last he approached a hedge and hopped right up to the place where a little doe hare sat refreshing herself with a rutabaga.

With a high, saluting hop he bowed low before the little mouse-grey thing. His eyes glittered and he shook with eagerness; he kissed the earth where her feet had trod. He made is best caper before her—his ears in continuous and sparkling conversation with her.

The little doe hare was something prudish. But Josse began to caress her and to touch her muzzle with his forepaws.

At last the little grey thing began to touch his.

Suddenly they noticed a creeping and wriggling in the earth beneath them and for a moment the attention of the suitor was distracted by a big earth-worm which had come toiling up now that the frost was over.

The worm, with no head and no tail, no legs and only a long string of flesh that was rounded at both ends, wriggled over the earth and hailed Josse on the borders of his new kingdom—for Josse had at last found his reason for going farther off from the fields he knew so well. The little doe hare was his reward for venturing beyond his natural surroundings, amid which, day by day, he had jogged on. He had struck out for himself to become cunning among the cunning—Lepidus's successor!